T0022411

PENGUIN BOOKS
SHUNYA

Born Mumtaz Ali in Thiruvananthapuram, Kerala, Sri M is a spiritual teacher, author, social reformer, educationist and global speaker. His memoir, *Apprenticed to a Himalayan Master: A Yogi's Autobiography*, published in 2011, became an instant bestseller; the sequel, *The Journey Continues*, was published in 2017.

He is the author of various other books on philosophy, yoga and Indian mysticism. Sri M established The Satsang Foundation twenty years ago and his mission has resulted in several initiatives in areas of education, community health, environment and the oneness of humanity.

Among the many awards and honours he has received, Sri M was conferred the Padma Bhushan by the Government of India in January 2020 for distinguished service of high order in spirituality.

Shunya

A NOVEL

SRI M

PENGUIN BOOKS

An imprint of Penguin Random House

PENGUIN BOOKS

USA | Canada | UK | Ireland | Australia
New Zealand | India | South Africa | China

Penguin Books is part of the Penguin Random House group of companies
whose addresses can be found at global.penguinrandomhouse.com

Published by Penguin Random House India Pvt. Ltd
4th Floor, Capital Tower 1, MG Road,
Gurugram 122 002, Haryana, India

Penguin
Random House
India

First published by Westland Publications Private Limited in 2018
This edition published in Penguin Books by Penguin Random House India in 2022

ISBN 9780143458609

Typeset in Garamond Regular by SURYA, New Delhi
Printed at Replika Press Pvt. Ltd, India

www.penguin.co.in

MIX
Paper from
responsible sources
FSC® C016779

1

For well over sixteen years, Sadasivan had to pass the old, abandoned cremation ground at midnight on his way back home from his toddy shop.

He prided himself on the fact that he didn't believe in ghosts and ghouls and other superstitions and yet, every time he passed the gate of the crematorium, an unknown fear gripped him and his hair stood on end.

That night, too, as he whizzed past the gate on his Royal Enfield motorbike—an upgrade from his old bicycle which he had felt took ages to clear the distance—Sadasivan followed the simple rule he had devised to make things easier: 'Don't look in the direction of the crematorium. Go as fast as you can.'

He had almost passed its gate when he distinctly heard a voice calling him out by name. Try as he might, he couldn't resist the temptation to turn and look. A shiver went up his spine.

A figure clad in white leapt out of the gate and, in the bright light of the solitary street lamp, Sadasivan could see him coming in his direction.

He lost control of his motorbike which hit a protruding flagstone, skid sideways, and sent him flying across the road.

As he picked himself up, he was scared stiff to see the white-robed figure right by his side.

'Umph! Not bad. No major damage, Sadasiva. Get up and go home. Don't be frightened. I am not a ghost, ha ha!'

Sadasivan got up, dusted his clothes and picked up the motorbike which had fallen a few metres away. The bike seemed fine except for a dent or two and one broken rear-view mirror. Then he noticed that the skin on both his elbows and his left knee had peeled off. No other damage.

The stranger followed him to the bike.

'Who the hell are you,' shouted Sadasivan, angrily, 'popping up from the cremation ground at midnight like a ghost? Haven't seen you in these parts and how do you know my name?'

'Sadasiva, I'll see you tomorrow at your toddy shop, okay? We'll talk then. Now go home and take care of yourself. There are no ghosts—go home.'

Sadasivan started his bike and rode home wondering who this crazy man was. He had seen him at close quarters: a single piece of unwashed white mundu was wrapped around his waist with an equally unwashed, loose cotton shirt; he was barefooted and fair-complexioned, with a pointed Ho Chi Minh beard. Who was he? Didn't Sadasivan notice a bamboo flute in his hand? Where did he spring from? He was certainly not a local and yet he spoke Malayalam. By the time he reached his house his anger had vanished and, for some strange reason, he was looking forward to seeing the stranger the next day.

In ten minutes he was home. His wife was shocked to see him injured. 'Fell off the bike,' he said and while she washed and dressed the wounds and served him dinner, he told her the story of the night's adventure. 'Very odd man, Bhavani,' he told her. 'Said he'll see me at the toddy shop tomorrow. And, for some mysterious reason, I am looking forward to seeing him.'

'Be careful,' said Bhavani after she'd had her dinner and they'd retired to the bedroom. 'Maybe he's a madman.'

'How can a madman know my name?' asked Sadasivan as he was falling asleep. He had taken a paracetamol and as the pain of his bruises slowly ebbed, sleep the ultimate reliever took over.

❧

Breakfast, one more paracetamol and a few bandaids later, Sadasivan was ready to go. As usual he rode to Toddy Shop No. 420 and opened it. Toddy shops are open all day but rush hour is usually after sunset.

Toddy has been, for hundreds of years, the favourite spirituous beverage of Malayalis and continues to have its committed adherents despite the influx of distilled spirits like rum and whiskey, which are referred to as 'Indian made foreign liquor'. A fermented alcoholic drink made from the sweet, milky sap that flows from the succulent new bud of the coconut palm when its tip is expertly snipped off, it is called 'kallu' in the local language.

More potent than beer, slightly sweet, with a musty odour and the colour of highly diluted milk, it is served in small licensed pubs called 'kallu shaaps' or toddy shops. Toddy shops are found in all corners of Kerala, especially in small towns, and unlike posh metropolitan pubs, are simple, thatched or tiled-roofed sheds managed usually by the owner himself, a cook or two and a couple of assistants.

Sadasivan waited eagerly the whole day. No sign of the madman. At sunset, 'Sada annan', or big brother Sada, never failed to offer incense before the pictures of the gods in his shop. He had just finished offering incense to the elephant-headed god Ganesha and the photo of Sri Narayana Guru, a holy man and social reformer, when he saw the strange man standing at the door. 'Why am I so excited?' he wondered to himself.

Examining him closely now, Sadasivan found him to be of medium height and well past middle-age. Time had toughened his face but wrinkles were few. He had sharp features and his once fair complexion was now sunburned to a reddish brown. He had long grey hair with a few black streaks, which he had gathered into a bun and secured on the crown of his head with a jute string.

Apart from the beard, he had a few long strands on his upper lip. With a clean shave he would have looked younger and handsome.

He was in the same outfit as he was the previous night—unwashed white mundu and shirt.

His large calloused feet were bare and he wore neither watch nor finger-ring, nor any of the paraphernalia of a wandering mendicant. Yet something about his demeanour, the calmness of his expression, and his dark, deep-set eyes made Sadasivan feel that he was facing a holy man, a sage, a man who *knew*. And then there was that mild fragrance of incense.

And yes, in his right hand he held an old-fashioned bamboo flute of the kind used by snake-charmers.

They looked at each other for a while. The strange man scrutinised him closely. His penetrating eyes darted swiftly from Sadasivan's dark, close-cropped hair to his chubby face which sported a coal-black, luxuriant handle-bar moustache, and further down to his tight, white, half-sleeved shirt, tailored more to show off the rippling muscles within than to cover the body, and his spotless white mundu with a bright red border. Then, in Malayalam, he said, 'Can I come in?' in an attractive voice, pleasant yet authoritative.

'Please come in,' said Sadasivan. 'You look like a Saami,

a wandering holy man. What's Saami's name? What should I call you?'

'You may call me what you like, but I call myself Shunya.'

Sadasivan scratched his head trying to understand the word. 'Shunya…Shunyam?…but Saami, shunyam means zero, nothing…'

'Yes, I am nothing, no-thing, no-body, zero-man— understood?'

He pointed at the picture of Narayana Guru. 'He was a great nothing: zero. You all have turned him into a small photograph. He was no-thing. I am no-thing. I am zero. You add zeros to make tens, hundreds, thousands, millions—all zeros, nothings.'

Sadasivan was trying to digest the words when the stranger interrupted, 'Can you give me some black tea?'

Sadasivan looked at him thoughtfully. He probably didn't have any money. Was he really a madman like Bhavani said? Who else will ask for black tea in a toddy shop, or, was he a wandering holy man? He remembered his mother saying that great saints sometimes pretended to be madmen. 'If you see a madman, son,' she used to say, 'feed him. He might be a holy man. Good luck will shine on you'.

The shop was empty anyway. 'Sit down, Saami,' he said, 'I'll get you some kattan chaaya. This, as you know, is a toddy shop but I'll get some kattan for you from the kitchen.'

'I am always drunk. No need for toddy, and add plenty of jaggery to the tea. I like it sweet.'

With that the stranger walked through the hall to the western end of the shop and went out of the small door into the little backyard as if he knew where he was going. An old, thatched, mud-walled cottage stood on one side beside a huge jackfruit tree. Jackfruits hung in abundance. Under its shade was a roughly hewn granite slab. He sat on it, cross-legged, like the Buddha.

'You like that seat, Saami?' Sadasivan asked.

'Yes. You don't mind, right?'

'No, Saami.'

Sadasivan shouted loudly at one of his waiters who was in the kitchen. 'Raghava, bring a glass of kattan for Saami. Add three spoons of jaggery instead of sugar. He is sitting here, near the cottage.'

'Whose cottage is this?' asked Shunya.

'Mine, Saami, but since I have built a house closer to the city, I keep it locked up. Both my servers and the cook live in the city. I am wondering if I should demolish it or do it up and rent it. Who is going to take an old, thatched mud house these days, and that too in the backyard of a toddy shop?'

'Nice place, hmph,' said Shunya.

The black tea arrived. Raghavan placed the glass on the stone slab and walked away without a word.

'Drink the tea, Saami,' said Sadasivan, 'and let me know if you want another glass. Anything to chew on?'

'No, nothing.'

Shunya took a noisy sip, looked up at the sky and said, 'First class.' Sadasivan went back to attend to his duties.

That evening the shop was full. Sadasivan was overjoyed. For the last three weeks, he had been going through a bad spell. He had even begun to think that the days of toddy shops were numbered. For Indian-made foreign liquor like whiskey, brandy, beer and the rest were getting more popular by the day.

But that day it was different. There were not enough seats for the customers. Sadasivan was convinced that it was all due to the Saami's blessings. He made sure that no customer went to the backyard and disturbed him. The longer he remained there, the better.

Shunya finished his tea. Then he walked through the shop, stood near the cash counter and said to Sadasivan, 'No money.'

Sadasivan stood up. 'It's a pleasure, Saami. You don't have to pay. Come again tomorrow.'

'We'll see,' he said and walked out before Sadasivan could even ask him where he could be found.

He could not stop thinking about Shunya even after he had closed the shop and gone home at 1 a.m. As he passed the crematorium on his mobike, he wondered if Shunya was sleeping there but didn't have the guts to investigate.

'Strange man,' he said to Bhavani, 'very stange man,' and related what had happened.

'Oh don't worry,' said Bhavani, 'he'll come back to you. I can feel it strongly.'

2

The following day was a Thursday. By evening, the shop was full, but there was no sign of Shunya. Sadasivan felt as though he was longing to see a dear friend. Even after he had wound up for the night and got on to his bike, he hoped Shunya would appear and ask for a drink. It was not to be.

He told Bhavani that night, 'See, you were wrong. The man never turned up.'

'I think he has worked some magic on you,' she teased him. 'Now shall we go to sleep or...?'

'I am a little tired. Let's sleep.'

'Okay.'

∾

On Friday evening, Shunya appeared at six. Sadasivan ran out eagerly to receive him.

'Saami, what happened yesterday? I waited for you.'

'Yes, yes, I know', said Shunya, 'you waited because your business did well. You felt Shunya brought you luck. Bloody fool!'

'No, Saami, it's not like that. Come and have a cup of tea.'

'Only one?'

'No, no, take as much as you want.'

'But I can't pay for it. I have no money.'

'It's on the house, Saami!'

Shunya walked towards the jackfruit tree in the

backyard and sat on the stone slab, which seemed to be his favourite seat.

Sadasivan called out, 'Raghava, Gopi, are you there? Bring a glass of kattan for Saami.'

The tea arrived, and Shunya drained half of it in one go. Sadasivan waited respectfully. He scratched the back of his head and stood quietly, wondering if he should talk.

'Umph, what is it?' asked Shunya.

'Have another glass of tea, Saami.'

'Yes, I will. Is that all?'

'And maybe you would like something to eat?...'

'I am hungry. Give me something to eat.'

'Saami, there is some lovely boiled tapioca and tasty...' Sadasivan bit his lip and stopped himself in time. He was going to say 'tasty matthi fish curry' but what if Shunya was a holy man who didn't touch meat or fish?

'Bring it. Tapioca and...?'

'Fish curry, but if you don't like that, then we have a nice coconut chamanthi.'

'Okay. Bring the tapioca, the fish curry, and the chamanthi, but very little of each. I eat everything. What comes out of your mouth is more important than what goes in. I eat when I am hungry. Go and bring the food.'

Sadasivan went into the kitchen and selected two big pieces of boiled tapioca, some fish curry and chamanthi. He put it all in one large steel plate and personally took it to Saami.

The shop was beginning to fill up.

'Raghava,' Sadasivan said as he walked out with the dish, 'you sit at the cash counter. Let Gopi and Thangappan look after the kitchen and the service. I am going to talk to that Saami out there. If anybody wants to see me, tell them I am busy. They must wait.'

'Why is he so caught up with that nut?' asked Gopi in a low voice, as soon as Sadasivan had gone out of the kitchen.

'Who knows?' said Raghavan, 'maybe he thinks that Saami has brought in some luck. The shop has been full since day before yesterday.'

'Wait till his wife Bhavaniamma catches up,' muttered Thangappan, 'Quite a handsome nut that Saami.'

'Shut up,' said Raghavan, 'always thinking of Bhavaniamma. He seems to be a holy man to me. If you are itching, you go try your luck with her sometime. Have you nothing else to think of but her? Granted, she looks like the actress Sheila, but still...'

'You shut up!' snapped Thangappan.

Sadasivan placed the food on the stone slab, and went back to the kitchen for a glass of water and some more tea.

'Saami, I am keeping the food here,' he said, 'call me if you need more.'

'Next time, serve me on a banana leaf,' said Shunya, 'I don't like steel plates.'

'Okay.'

Sadasivan hovered around, wondering how to open the conversation.

'You want to speak to me?' Shunya asked.

'Yes, Saami.'

'Go ahead.'

'Saami, I know it will be too much to ask who you are and where you come from and all that since you say you are Shunya,' Sadasivan blurted out, 'but something pulls me towards you. I feel I must take care of you.'

'Who knows where you sleep or what you eat. See this cottage? I used to live here before I rented a house in Poojapura. With just a little bit of doing up, it will become habitable. If you don't mind, why don't you stay here? You don't have to do anything. Just stay. The toddy shop's kitchen will provide you food, and you can drink as much kattan as you like. No conditions, no strings attached—only please don't say no. I haven't yet asked Bhavani, my wife, but I know her well. She will not object. Please let me look after you.'

Inexplicably, tears filled up Sadasivan's eyes. On an impulse, he, who had never bowed his head to anyone other than their patron saint Narayan Guru, bent down and touched Shunya's feet. 'Live here, please, Saami!'

'That's enough! I'll come back tomorrow and reside here in this cottage for as long as I want to. When I feel like going away, I'll leave. You shouldn't then search for me. I'll eat only one meal a day and that will be in the evening. Is that fine with you?'

'Yes, Saami.'

'And I will meet or talk to people only if I wish to, except you.'

'Okay, Saami.'

'You can bring me some kattan along with my food, unless I specifically ask you not to.'

'Done, Saami.'

Shunya finished the food in a hurry, drank the tea in two or three gulps, and belched loudly.

He stood up and shouted thrice, '*Annam Brahman.*' With that, he walked out of Toddy Shop No. 420.

'Tomorrow I will see you,' he said as he left. The time was 9.30 p.m.

'Who was that?' asked one of the customers.

'God knows. Some nut,' said another.

'We'll ask Sada anna,' said a third.

By the time they left, they were so drunk that they forgot to ask.

Sadasivan went home that night and told his wife all that had happened. 'See, I told you that he would be back,' she said. 'But what about Monday? The shop will be closed, so what will he eat?'

'God!' said Sadasivan, 'I forgot about that. Maybe I should take him some food from home on Monday evening, along with some black tea. Tomorrow morning, ask Nanoo and Lila to do up the cottage. The roof is fine. Got it re-thatched two months ago, remember? The place just needs to be cleaned and the floor plastered with cow dung.'

'All right, now why don't you have a bath and eat, and then...'

'And then?'

'Oh come on, don't embarrass me.'

'...Give me some coconut oil.'

While Bhavani waited for her husband, a strange feeling crept into her heart. It was as if the fulfilment she had been seeking ever since their marriage was just round the corner. For the ten years they had been married—she at twenty and he at thirty—they had tried everything, but she couldn't conceive. The doctors kept saying that there was nothing wrong with them, but it seemed like there was no hope.

Allopathy, Ayurveda, siddha, homeopathy, mantra, tantra, voodoo, nothing had worked, but now, just now, a mysterious hope seemed to have taken root. Was it in some way linked to this odd stranger her husband was talking about? An image of herself breastfeeding a baby suddenly flashed in her mind's eye and vanished in a second.

'Bhavani, what are you dreaming of?' whispered Sadasivan in her ear.

Startled, she replied, 'I was just thinking of your Saami.'

3

The next evening, Shunya arrived at five-thirty. He carried with him a small, grey cloth bundle, an old copper mug, and the flute Sadasivan had seen with him on the first day. These were his sole possessions. 'God knows what's in that bundle,' Sadasivan thought to himself.

He had arrived early that day and made sure everything was in order. Leela, the maid, had neatly plastered the floor with cow dung and drawn beautiful rangoli designs with white rice flour. The palm leaf sleeping mat was clean, and a fresh, clean pillow was placed at one end of it. The clay water pot was filled with water and an aluminium tumbler stood beside it. Sadasivan had also ensured that the single electric light had a new bulb placed in the holder.

Shunya entered the cottage without a word, set down his luggage, and peeped into the unused kitchen. Apparently satisfied, he smiled for the first time.

It was a kind smile, and it seemed to come straight from the heart. But after a second, the neutral expression returned.

'Umph,' he said, 'this is fine for me. You have done your work, go now. At six-thirty, give me my daily rations.'

'Yes, Saami.'

Sadasivan stepped out of the cottage. Shunya shut the door after him.

And so, from that day, Shunya Saami began to live in the cottage in the backyard of Toddy Shop No. 420.

He remained inside the cottage for most of the day, except in the morning when he went out to relieve himself in the bushes beyond the lush paddy fields, or to have his bath in the pond of the abandoned Shiva temple. In the evening, he would be found sitting cross-legged on the stone slab under the jackfruit tree. There, he would eat his only meal of the day, and drink his kattan chaaya.

Nobody knew what he did inside the cottage during the day. At night, they thought he slept, but Gopi, the cook, swore that late one night, when he had passed the cottage after attending a funeral, he had heard strange voices coming from inside, talking in an undecipherable language.

Nobody paid much attention to his story. One month passed by.

∾

Meanwhile, important changes were taking place in Sadasivan's life. In a property dispute case, the judgement was ruled in his favour. His business improved. The Travancore Rural Bank came forward to give him a low-interest loan to develop his farmland. For the first time, he had enough money to buy himself a good second-hand Fiat Elegant and he started taking driving lessons. He finalised plans to build his own house. And with all this, his devotion to Saami grew by the day.

Some people were curious about this new fixture at Toddy Shop No. 420. Could he be the reason why fortune was beginning to shine on Sadasivan? 'Coincidence, mere coincidence,' said the pragmatic materialists; 'divine blessings,' said the religious; 'he is just a mad man,' said the intellectuals who had only finished high school. By and large, the toddy shop veterans, Sadasivan's regular customers, kept away from Shunya. They didn't want their toddy-induced alcoholic euphoria to be diluted by any religious or spiritual opiate which this strange holy man probably dispensed.

Sadasivan, however, protected Shunya from the inquisitive. He took care to see that no one disturbed him. He met Shunya only once a day and served him food and black tea. His attempts to thank him or start any conversation were always cut short by a curt 'Umph. Now you can go.'

Raghavan, Gopi and Thangappan saw him a few times while serving food or tea, but there was very little conversation except the occasional 'Good fish.'

'Shall I bring more?'

'No, no, bring some more tea.'

'Saami, want a beedi?'

'No.'

But it was different when Bhavani came with her husband.

It was 6.15 p.m. As they got off Sadasivan's motorbike, they heard the music. Intense, undulating, soulful strains of the flute. As they approached the cottage, Sadasivan said, 'I think Saami is playing his flute. Ah! How beautiful!'

'Ssh!' whispered Bhavani, 'Don't talk so loudly. Oh! So beautiful.'

By then, they were in front of the cottage. The door was closed. The music continued from within. Bhavani sank to the floor and closed her eyes in ecstasy. Sadasivan sat down beside her. He felt an unfamiliar, sweet sensation in his heart and hoped that the music wouldn't end.

But it did. The door opened and Shunya stood before them. A rare smile lit up his countenance. He said, 'So you brought your wife along.'

'Yes, Saami, she wanted to come.'

Bhavani opened her eyes and they both stood up. 'Come,' said Shunya, and went and occupied his stone seat under the jackfruit tree.

'Bring the food here and come sit down, both of you.'

'Saami, we would prefer to stand.'

'Ah! Bhavani,' Shunya addressed her.

'Yes,' said Bhavani.

'Shankar Mahadev, the great god of the yogis, powerful consort of the Lord, Bhavani, Bhayankari,' chanted Shunya. His eyes rolled upwards until only the whites were visible. 'No progeny. Pray to the Lord of your heart. You have Krishna's picture at home, no?'

'Yes, Saami,' Bhavani's eyes filled with tears. A lump formed in her throat, and she could barely speak.

Shunya jumped up and ran to a hibiscus plant that stood a little distance away from the cottage. He plucked a red, fully blossomed flower and ran back to give it to Bhavani. 'Take this and offer it to your Krishna. Wait patiently. I am nothing. Zero, Boojyam, Shunya. Goddess Bhavani is allowed only once a month here. Now go and don't tell anybody about anything I told you.' Suddenly, he looked furious and insisted, 'Go, go!'

They left, and kept all that had happened to themselves. Back home, every time Bhavani looked at Lord Krishna's picture, she saw Shunya's face instead, smiling, not furious, and heard the music deep within her soul.

༄

And so Shunya lived on, safe from the public gaze, until the fateful arrival of Kuttimana Kunjan Namboodiri, the great Vedic scholar, tantric and astrologer, reputed to be an expert at curing snake-bites with mantras. He was invited to visit the dilapidated Shiva temple beside which lay the pond in which Shunya had his daily bath.

He was asked to divine how the old temple, once established by an ancient Namboodiri Brahmin family, could be revived and the Linga, a symbol of God Shiva, be re-consecrated. About a hundred people, including the president of the local Village Administrative Committee, accompanied Kunjan Namboordiri when he arrived.

The Namboodiri Brahmins are peculiar to Kerala. Legends say that they were brought from the north by Parasurama, the axe-wielding Brahmin incarnation of the great god Mahavishnu, and settled in the land reclaimed by him from the ocean. It is said that he cast his divine axe into the sea, and the sea receded, exposing the land which is now believed to be Kerala.

At one time, the Namboodiri Brahmins were worshipped as 'gods on earth' by the general populace. They considered themselves the highest among Brahmins and looked down even upon Brahmins of other sects, especially the ones from neighbouring Tamil Nadu. Their word was law, and they owned vast tracts of land. Many among them were renowned Sanskrit scholars and experts on tantric magic. Snake worship was an important part of their expertise and some were famous for their hypnotic power over snakes. But all that was history.

By the 1960s the Namboodiri joint facilities called illams had, by and large, degenerated. Some of the descendants of illustrious Namboodiri clans turned to communism, who leaned towards the Marx-Engels-Lenin trinity instead of the divine trinity of the creator god Brahma, the preserver god Vishnu and the destroyer god Maheshwar, whom their ancestors had worshipped.

Yet there were, here and there, a few Namboodiris who still retained their reputation and Kuttimana Kunjan Namboodiri was one of them. He was believed to be thorough in his knowledge of the Vedas and Upanishads, and in music, dance, astrology, temple construction and the science of serpents.

Tirumaeni, the Great One, as Namboodiris were traditionally addressed in Kerala, squatted on a straw mat in the courtyard of the ruined temple, surrounded by all the men and women who had accompanied him. After drawing the magic diagrams on the sand in front of him with his index finger, he shook the little sea shells called kavadi, which he held in his right fist, and threw them like dice on the squares he had drawn. Then he began to chant.

He had just finished chanting 'Hail Ganesha, the elephant headed God' in a sonorous voice when an enormous brown cobra, nearly six feet long, came rushing out of a large hole near the temple's courtyard and headed towards the gathering.

'Pamboo, snake!' someone shouted and the crowd scattered. Meenakshi, a young school teacher, was frozen with fear. She sat where she was, a horrified expression on her face. The only other person left was Kunjan Namboodiri himself who remained glued to his seat, looking as petrified as the girl.

The cobra stopped in front of the girl, raised its head and expanded its hood, showing off the yellow scissor mark, and hissed. Then it swiftly struck her twice on her left thigh and made for the Namboodiri.

She screamed and fell unconscious.

The Namboodiri, who was beginning to chant a mantra, jumped up and started running, with the snake in hot pursuit. He was almost near the pond when he stumbled and fell.

Shunya had just climbed up the steps of the pond after his bath when he saw the Namboodiri fall. The snake halted, raised its hood, swayed and hissed. It was getting ready to strike its next victim.

The Namboodiri trembled in fear. Death stood before him in the form of the cobra.

Shunya calmly walked in a circle, and as deftly as a cat, crept behind the cobra. With a sudden movement of his right hand, he had the cobra's head and neck firmly gripped in his right fist. He pulled up the struggling reptile, and with his other hand holding its lashing tail, walked into the Sarpa Kaavu, the serpent's grove, which was adjacent to the temple.

Sarpa Kaavus are small, thickly wooded groves dedicated to snakes. They are the remnants of Kerala's sepent-worshipping days when snakes were considered gods. These groves were the snakes' habitat, tended by humans to appease the snake gods. No one killed snakes in the groves. One entered at one's own risk.

Within minutes, Shunya came out of the grove, minus the serpent. Even before the onlookers had recovered from the shock, he was kneeling near the unconscious girl and checking her pulse and eyes. Saliva dripped from the sides of her mouth. Some of those who had run away now came back. One person said, 'Right thigh. That's where I saw it bite.'

Shunya raised her body and propped it against a broken wall. He then stretched her right leg and pulled up the saree. He looked carefully for the snakebite. 'Nothing here,' he said and continued to search for it, and then exclaimed, 'Ah! Here it is in the ankle. I found it.' Putting his mouth to the swollen reddish marks left by the fangs of the cobra, he started sucking the blood.

He spat out a mouthful, sucked again, and continued the process three or four times. The girl opened her eyes, shuddered, and said, 'Where am I?'

'Here, with these cowards,' said Shunya. Then, raising his voice he shouted, 'Who had come with this girl?'

A middle-aged man came forward and replied, 'I am her brother, Saami.'

'Take her home. She is fine, but don't let her sleep for four hours. Give her plenty of coconut water. Go now.'

Shunya then turned to the Namboodiri who had calmed himself down and was sitting on the stone bench near the pond. The Namboodiri started to say something but was cut short by Shunya's loud and clear voice.

'Son of a kazuvaeri.'

Kunjan Namboodiri blinked and said nothing. Kazuvaeri in Malayalam was a vile abuse. Shunya sat down beside him.

'Insulted? Do you know what it means?'

He turned to the crowd which had regrouped and addressed the president of the Village Administrative Committee, who was a local politician, 'O President, why don't you bring me some black tea? My mouth is dry.'

He turned again to Kunjan Namboodiri. 'What have you achieved with your mantras and Vedas? Fearlessness is the sign of enlightenment. You pretend. Don't pretend. Be truthful.'

Someone came with a glass of black tea. Shunya emptied the glass in no time and put it away. 'Umph, that was great. So, what was I saying? Oh yes, about kazuvaeri, you know what a kazugu is, don't you? The crowbar-like sharp tool fixed to the ground used for de-husking coconuts. One of the punishments meted out to thieves and adulterers in the old days, to the great pleasure of the rulers, was to make them sit on the pointed end of the kazugu. Hence, 'kazugu-aeri', one who climbed the kazugu. The result? It would, by the sheer weight of the body, go right up the arse and into the stomach.

'If none of your ancestors were thieves or adulterers, say so.'

'No,' replied Kunjan Namboodiri, still struggling to regain his composure, 'none, as far as I know.'

Shunya stood up and said, 'Oh Tirumaeni! Deep regret for using a swear word. You're not a bad fellow except that you got scared. If you feel like talking to me sometime, about philosophy, tantra, or anything you like, drop by at my abode, which is sanctified by the coconut nectar, toddy. See that toddy shop there, no. 420? Ask Sadasivan and he'll let you in. I may choose to talk or remain silent. Come only after seven in the evening. I am warning you though that it is no place for a dignified person like you. It is full of drunkards. I am a drunkard too, in my own way. Go now. May the peace of Shunya, the Void, descend on you.'

4

Two days later, at seven-thirty in the evening, Kunjan Namboodiri showed up at the toddy shop. Sadasivan stood up respectfully.

'Don't bother to stand up,' said the Namboodiri. 'Ask Saami if I can see him.'

Sadasivan went in to check, and returned to lead Kunjan Namboodiri to the stone slab under the jackfruit tree.

'Sit down, Great One,' said Shunya, 'Sadasiva, bring me my black tea, my soma.'

That was the beginning of what later came to be known as the toddy shop satsangs. For quite some time, until Shunya disappeared as mysteriously as he had come, the satsangs continued. People would gather to debate, argue, criticise, or merely listen. Some came simply out of curiosity and some came to catch a glimpse of Shunya, whom they believed to be a holy sage, to seek his blessings.

'I want to ask you a question,' said Kunjan Namboodiri.

'No, you don't. Just listen.'

Sadasivan appeared with the kettle and poured out a glass of black tea.

'Leave the kettle here and go,' instructed Shunya. 'Brahmin, will you have some nectar, the sacred soma?'

'No, I don't drink tea.'

'As you wish.'

'Tea causes indigestion for me. Too much gas builds up and I feel like vomiting.'

'It is good to vomit sometimes. Clears up the muck. Don't you chant the Gayatri Mantra every day? "May my

23

intelligence be stimulated." Dangerous! I chanted it daily as a child and see the result? I am crazy. Ha, ha, the sober are sane. The lover is insane. But you don't know "love", do you?'

'I can't say really, but my question, Saami...'

'Wait, tirumeni, impatience is no good,' Shunya cut him short. Raising his glass, he finished the tea, and smacked his lips. He filled the glass again and placed it on the slab by his side.

'Ah! That was good. Fresh black tea smells good, like the first summer rain. What a great concoction the Chinese invented: chai! Okay, now, what were you saying?'

'Saami, you seem to know how to handle snakes. If you know the secrets of the hooded serpents, the Nagas, will you teach me?'

'Ah! The Nagas...First, listen to this story of the naked ones. Five naked men decided to walk across a river. They were stark naked, with not a stitch on them, like new-born babies. But there was one condition: no one's private parts should get wet. Not a drop of water. So they stood in a line, one behind the other, their bodies so close that their private parts were hidden perfectly in the...'

'I refuse to listen to such crap,' said Kunjan Namboodiri, standing up.

'Ah! Shocked? Revolted? Doesn't every man have it? A child is born because of it, and every man except the celibate uses it for profit or pleasure, but you don't like the word. Dirty, is it? The cultured will not utter it. It is anathema to you.

'You have probably never heard of Edward Bulwer Lytton who in 1839 said, "the pen-is mightier than the sword". Battles have been fought for its sake. Relax, I can see your face turning red. But I am digressing—let me get back to the story.

'So, as I was saying, five naked men wanted to cross the river without wetting their…'

'No, I am not going to listen to this!'

'Ok, now tell me, have you gone to Prayag during Kumbha Mela? No, you haven't. So you haven't seen the Naga sadhus going for a holy dip in the confluence of the three rivers, proud of what nature has endowed them with. The Digambar Jain monks are not ashamed of their nakedness either. They say that one who has shame is far from Nirvana. Do you still think I am talking crap?'

'Yes, I do,' said the Namboodiri with a sneer, 'and anyway, if you fancy that you have attained Nirvana, how come you are fully clad? Enough of this nonsense! I need to leave.'

Kunjan Namboodiri turned to walk away when he heard a stern command, 'Stop, Brahmin!' He felt a strange force arresting his steps. 'Turn around,' said Shunya. The Namboodiri obeyed.

The first thing he saw was that Shunya was standing naked. A garland of pure white lotus flowers hung around his waist. Then he saw something that filled him with intense fear. Coiled around Shunya's right thigh was a large, hissing black serpent with its hood spread, and it appeared to the Namboodiri that it was getting ready to strike him.

With a loud, terror-stricken cry, Kunjan Namboodiri turned and bolted. Heading straight for the door of the toddy shop, he ran into the street, jumped inside an autorickshaw, and directed the rickshaw driver to take him home. Rajan, the auto driver, noticed that Kunjan

Namboodiri, whom he was acquainted with, looked agitated. What was a teetotaller like him doing in a toddy shop, thought Rajan, but he refrained from asking him anything. 'None of my business,' he said to himself.

༆

Sadasivan was leaving the kitchen when he heard a loud cry coming from the direction of Shunya's cottage. Then he saw the Namboodiri rushing past him. Concerned about Shunya's safety, he hurried towards the cottage.

He saw Shunya sitting on the stone slab, smiling to himself. He was clad in his usual mundu and half-sleeved shirt. Perplexed, Sadasivan enquired, 'Are you all right, Saami? I heard a scream.'

'All fine here. That Namboodiri screamed. Something seems to have frightened him.'

'Shall I bring you some food? Or tea?'

'No, I am not hungry. You go back to work. I am turning in for the night.' With a chuckle, Shunya walked into the cottage. Sadasivan went back to count the cash, still wondering about the scream.

༆

By the time he reached home, Kunjan Namboodiri managed to calm himself down. His wife, Ambika, who served him a dinner of konji, parippu and pappadam, noticed that he spoke less than usual. She thought that he must be tired.

'Ambi, I am a little tired. I am going to sleep now. Finish your dinner and come,' he said, and went into the bedroom.

Entering the bedroom after dinner, Ambika found that he had already fallen asleep, which was unusual. 'Something doesn't seem right. I'll ask him in the morning when he wakes up,' Ambika thought to herself and lay down carefully on the bed, making sure not to disturb her husband.

Around midnight Kunjan Namboodiri screamed, 'Snake, snake!' in his sleep and was woken up by his wife. He sat up and rubbed his eyes. 'Terrible dream,' he said, 'I dreamt that Shunya, that mad fellow who lives in Sadasivan's toddy shop, has turned into a massive blue-coloured cobra and is coming to get me. Shiva, Shiva!'

'It's all right, it's just a dream,' said Ambika. 'Go to sleep now. Shall I bring you some water to drink? No? Okay, go to sleep. I wanted to tell you to not visit that strange fellow. I didn't because you wouldn't have listened to me. You never do. Go to sleep now and tell me what happened in the morning.'

Kunjan Namboodiri fell into a deep sleep. In the morning, he told his wife about his meeting with Shunya and how he had stood naked before him with a black cobra coiled around his thigh.

'Don't go there again,' Ambika pleaded. 'Maybe he is a black magician. What a crude fellow.'

'I won't go,' said Kunjan Namboodiri, but after a few days, he did.

5

Meanwhile, others began to visit Sadasivan's toddy shop. Meenakshi, the school teacher who would have died from the snakebite if Shunya hadn't intervened, came to see him one evening. Women, as a rule, never entered toddy shops, even in this stronghold of dialectical materialism. She had to be taken to Shunya's presence through the back door.

'He may seem a little crazy,' warned Sadasivan, 'but I think he's harmless. Gopi, take her to Saami.'

Shunya was drinking his black tea when she arrived. He sent Gopi away.

'Sit down, girl. The cigars were lovely. Churchill loved them. How old are you?'

Meenakshi faltered. She thought that he was really crazy, uttering meaningless words. The question about her age was the only thing she understood. 'I am twenty-three, Saami,' she said, 'but I don't understand what you mean by "cigars" and "Churchill".' 'I actually came to thank you,' she added quickly, 'you saved my life.'

'It was just sheer luck that you were saved. You are a teacher, right? Ah! You should know about Churchill's cigars, and expand the horizons of your mind. You have heard of Winston Churchill?'

'Yes, Saami. He was the British prime minister during the World War and well known for his wit. He was also a great orator, I have read.'

'Yes, yes. You know history, young lady? You must be wondering how Shunya, the Void, knows all this. He doesn't. Shunya's state is like a clear slate. Thoughts come in, and then they are erased. They leave no trace.

'Anyway, Churchill, when he was posted in Madras as a junior officer in the British Indian Army, found that the cigars manufactured in Tiruchi had a special flavour which he loved. He was convinced that it had something to do with the dark-skinned damsels who made them by rolling the tobacco leaves on their thighs. Tiruchi cigars remained one of his all-time favourites. So, did you come only to thank me?'

Meenakshi hesitated and said, 'Yes, Saami, actually... no, Saami. I don't know how to begin. I...'

'Ha! You are in love. I can see it in your eyes.'

Meenakshi burst into tears. Shunya remained silent. After a while, she wiped her face dry and said, 'Saami, I love Salim, the son of the maulvi of the Paritala mosque. He loves me too. But there is no way we can get married. He doesn't want me to become a Muslim and I don't want him to become a Hindu. Can't one "human being" marry another, Saami?'

'Yes, you can. Go for a court marriage. Both of you are majors.'

'Saami, they will kill us, his people and mine. There is no one to help us.'

'I'll help you, you silly girl. The "Void" will help you.'

Meenakshi started to cry again.

'Stop crying, child, stay calm and listen. What does Salim do for a living?'

'Drawing teacher, Saami, he works in the same school where I teach science.'

'Good! Go tomorrow to the sub-registrar's office in Thiruvananthapuram and fix a date for your marriage registration. Take your boy with you. Ask a good friend to be witness. Do it quietly, without any fanfare, then come to see me. Be brave. Go now.'

'I'll take my friend, Mathew. I am sure he'll come.' She then bent down to touch Shunya's feet.

'Dear girl, don't tug at my legs. Why prostrate before the "Void"? Go home, and talk to your lover boy.'

Meenakshi left.

'Sadasiva, send me something to eat,' Shunya called out.

Sadasivan appeared with a kettle of black tea and a tiffin carrier. He said, 'I bow to you, Saami. My wife sent you some idlis and chutney powder. Will you eat it?'

'Aah! Good, leave it here.'

'And Saami, it seems that girl, Meenakshi, who came to see you, is in love with a Muslim boy, Salim, the son of the maulvi of the Paritala mosque. I heard the maulvi has threatened to kill his son if he continued this relationship. I know Meenakshi's father. He says he will kill himself if she marries this boy.'

'Sadasiva, I told her to get married at the registrar's office.'

'Keep it to yourself for the time being, Saami! Don't let anyone know that you advised her, please. They'll come for you, Saami. You are my father, mother and Guru, Saami. Why did you do this?'

'Don't worry, Sadasiva, everything will be fine. What did your great saint Narayana Guru say? "One religion, one caste and one God for humanity as a whole." Do you fools practise it? Go now and do your work. Give your thirsty customers more toddy, the great equaliser. Let them drown their sorrows of inequality. *Paramanandam, paramanandam*, great joy, great joy!'

6

Meenakshi married Salim at the marriage registrar's office on Monday, the 25th of February, at 11 a.m. Mathew, the maths teacher, was witness and best man for both the bride and the groom. As they stepped out of the registrar's office, they ran into Madhavankutty Nair, Meenakshi's uncle, her mother's eldest brother who was a seventy-year-old bachelor.

'Meena,' he said in his gruff, authoritarian tone, 'what are you up to?'

He was six-foot tall, ramrod straight, and dark complexioned. With his trimmed, slightly upturned moustache, aquiline nose, square jaw and close-cropped silver hair, he looked quite stern. Clad in a mundu and white cotton shirt, with sleeves rolled up to the elbows, M.K., as he was popularly known, was a senior Marxist leader. He was reputed to be an expert in kalaripayattu, the martial art of Kerala.

Meenakshi trembled silently in fear. Salim tried to put up a brave front. 'We just got married at the registrar's,' he blurted out, looking down.

'Hey, Mathew,' said M.K., 'what is he saying?'

Mathew plucked up enough courage to say, 'Uncle, Meenakshi and Salim just got married at the registrar's office. Their parents were against it, so they had to do it secretly. I...'

'Enough,' said M.K. There was a short silence before he spoke again. His expression turned tender and he touched Meenakshi's head as he said, 'Brave girl. Well done, Salim! Somebody has to do away with all this nonsense.

'Meena, if you were in love with this young fellow, why didn't you tell me? I would have done something about it. Now who is going to console your mother or this fellow's father, the maulvi?'

Meena burst out crying. M.K. held her in his arms and consoled her. 'Okay, okay, now where are the two of you going to live?'

'I have rented a small house for them in Poojapura,' Mathew said.

'No, no, you must live with me at my house in Jagathy,' said M.K., 'Nobody will dare trouble you there. Come, let's get an auto-rickshaw. How many days have you two taken leave for?'

'Four days,' they said together.

'Then go to Kanyakumari tomorrow and enjoy the sea breeze for a day or two.'

They hired two auto-rickshaws. Meena and Salim got into one, Mathew and M.K. got into the other, and they drove to M.K.'s house.

'Good boy,' said M.K., patting Mathew's back, 'a friend in need, yeah? But tell me, how did Meena have the guts to take this decision? She was always so meek—or so I thought.'

'Shunya Saami,' said Mathew. 'He calls himself Shunya, the Void. Meena says he told her to go ahead and she was filled with infinite strength. I haven't met him, but Meena adores him. He saved her from almost certain death when the cobra bit her, you know.'

'I heard about that. I was away in Tellicherry organising a protest march. Shanta, Meena's mother, said something about it. That guy who they say lives in Sadasivan's toddy shop, right? Thought he must be one of those fake sadhus who makes a living out of fooling people. Parasites! But this is interesting. Maybe I should go meet this fellow.'

7

Being Meena's mother's eldest brother, M.K., following the matriarchal tradition, was the head of the family—a position of great authority. Moreover, the power he wielded as a senior member of the Communist Party, and the respect the general public had for his character and integrity helped him sort out Meena's problems within a month—or so it appeared.

Mohammed Maulvi, Salim's father, after a prolonged discussion with M.K., raised his hands in resignation and said with tears in his eyes, 'It is Allah's will. May Allah protect them. Nair saar, tell me where they live and I'll go and see them. They should not come here. It would be too risky.'

Later, he visited them in secret and blessed them with tears in his eyes.

Meena's parents and other family members, after a great deal of heated discussion and much crying and gnashing of teeth, ultimately let go of their resentment and invited the couple to stay in their family home.

But, deep down, under the seemingly still waters, attempts were afoot to fan the flames of hatred. What happened immediately afterwards added fuel to the fire.

∾

An evangelist by the name of Father Samuel, who said he was trained in America, came to preach in Thiruvananthapuram. Many people attended his revival meetings. Some claimed that the father had cured them of incurable diseases. News spread that the blind could see and the crippled could walk when the evangelist prayed and laid his hands on them. A small number of people became 'born-again' Christians. Ouseph, a minor village-level politician, was Father Samuel's agent. His secret stash in the bank grew day by day.

Ouseph was in charge of two things: one, gathering as many believers as possible and, two, recruiting people willing to act sick who, after a series of frenzied singing and prayers, would pretend to be cured when Father Samuel laid his hands on their heads and blessed them. Ouseph paid them handsomely from the money Samuel provided.

The drama was going on so well that the coffers were filling up fast from the offerings of the devout, apart from the dollars that flowed in from America. Father Samuel was very generous to Ouseph.

A shrewd fellow, Ouseph had identified two important factors which might interfere with the cash flow. The Catholic Church which was opposed to what they called 'renegade evangelists' was one, and he was working out a long-term plan to tackle that. The other was Shunya, believed to be some sort of a guru who had arrived from nowhere one fine day and now lived in the cottage behind Sadasivan's toddy shop.

There were many different reports on him. Some said he was a lunatic, others said he was a saint, an Avadhuta, and some others said that he was an imposter of some sort. Ouseph would have liked to agree with the last opinion, but whatever he was, Ouseph was convinced that he could prove to be a worse adversary than the Catholic Church.

Rumours were rife that it was Shunya who had arranged

the marriage between the school teacher Meenakshi and the maulvi's son. What if he influenced the Christian youth to intermarry? Meenakshi's friend, Mathew, was already very excited about this fellow. He had also heard that M.K. Nair, the veteran communist, was planning to meet Shunya. But more than all that, what troubled Ouseph was that his popularity seemed to be increasing day by day. Shunya could turn out to be quite a formidable obstacle to Ouseph's steadily increasing bank balance, considering that he seemed to have made derogatory references to Father Samuel to a couple of people. Shunya had to be tackled as quietly as possible.

Ouseph was almost certain that Shunya was an imposter and he thought he knew how to deal with him. Money was the answer. All imposters were greedy for money. There were no exceptions.

ॐ

So, one evening, Ouseph went to Sadasivan's Toddy Shop No. 420 and requested a meeting with Shunya Saami. He had come prepared with a lot of cash in the jute bag slung across his right shoulder. Sadasivan ushered him into Shunya's presence.

As soon as Sadasivan left, Ouseph got down to business. He introduced himself, 'I am Ouseph, I am in public service, and I also work for Father Samuel, the evangelist.'

'Oho,' said Shunya, 'and what have you come here for?'

Ouseph didn't mince his words. He said, 'I have come to negotiate a deal with you.' Taking out the cash from his bag, he laid it out in front of Shunya. He continued, 'All yours, Saami, five thousand rupees. Just do me a favour.

Ask your followers to go to Evangelist Samuel. You must have heard of him. Tell them he is a really great saint and please quit criticising him. Simple, isn't it? And I can bring you more money later. What say you?'

'You bastard!' said Shunya, 'I have not only heard of Samuel, I know much more about him and about you. I have my sources. I know he pays you to procure people for him. I know how he trains them to act like the blind, the crippled, and the possessed, who then pretend to be cured at his prayer meetings. I know where his money comes from, and more than that, I know what he does in his bedroom. Tell me, how much does he pay you for procuring young boys for his pleasure?'

'How much money do you want to keep your mouth shut, you crazy man?' pleaded Ouseph, shocked, angry and agitated. 'We can strike a bargain. Come on, tell me.'

'Shunya wants nothing but the Truth, and as for the money, take it and shove it up your arse. And don't come back again.'

'We'll see what happens,' said Ouseph, clenching his teeth, his face red with rage. Then picking up the money, he rushed out. Shunya hurled a stone after him yelling, 'Don't come back!'

By an odd coincidence, the very next day, the police raided Father Samuel's residence and caught him naked with a twelve-year-old orphan boy. The police claimed to have conducted the raid based on information provided by an anonymous telephone call. Samuel, who claimed he was merely blessing the boy, was arrested, but let out on bail, with further investigation pending. He jumped bail and quietly vanished from the scene.

Fortunately for Ouseph, though many people knew

about his association with Father Samuel, there was no concrete evidence which could be used against him in a court of law. However, Ouseph was convinced that Shunya was somehow responsible for Samuel's arrest, as well as for his own woes, financial and otherwise. On top of that, whenever he thought of how Shunya had insulted him on that day, he could feel the fire of anger coursing through his veins. He had to retaliate in some way. But what intrigued him was how the old fellow knew about Father Samuel's homosexual activities. For a second, he suspected Shunya was a CID sleuth in disguise, but he dismissed the thought. Shunya seemed to be raving mad. It was probably just clever guess work. Whatever it was, Ouseph was convinced he was to be dealt with.

He knew others who disliked Shunya intensely, and decided to approach them to discuss the matter seriously. A plan had to be worked out carefully, because the adversary looked crazy but was no fool.

Meanwhile, M.K. decided to meet Shunya. He was curious as to how someone who, from the information he had gathered, seemed to be a madman, was able to inspire so much courage in his usually shy niece. The meeting turned out to be interesting.

When Sadasivan saw M.K. approaching the toddy shop one evening, he became anxious. Would M.K. cause harm to his dear Saami? His fears were put to rest when M.K. walked up to him and said with a smile, 'Sadasiva, don't worry. I have only come to meet this man called Shunya. I appreciate the moral support he gave my niece, Meena. I am not about to become a devotee because I think all sadhus are frauds or just insane. How's business these days?'

'M.K. sir, you haven't come here for so long. Please come in,' said Sadasivan. 'Can I get you some toddy?'

M.K. went in and sat on one of the benches.

'Okay, I'll have a glass. Meanwhile, find out if your Shunya Saami will see me.'

Sadasivan brought him some toddy, placed it on the table, and went to Shunya.

He came back looking worried. 'Sir, he says he never sees anybody before seven. I told him who you are but he wouldn't listen. He just kept saying, "Seven o'clock, seven o'clock, ask him to wait." I am sorry, sir, I...'

M.K. smiled. 'Interesting,' he said, 'I'll wait and have another glass. But don't tell me anything about Shunya. I don't want to be prejudiced, this way or that.'

Sadasivan hurriedly took rice, avial and sambar for Shunya, who ate the food without a word. Sadasivan waited silently. After Shunya had finished his meal and burped loudly, Sadasivan said, 'M.K. saar is waiting to see you, Saami.'

'Seven o'clock,' he said again.

At precisely seven o'clock, Shunya called out loudly, 'Sadasiva, ask him to come.'

Sadasivan led M.K. to Shunya.

M.K., without any hesitation, sat down on the ground facing Shunya who sat on his usual stone slab.

'Sadasiva, bring me some black tea,' said Shunya, and then spoke to M.K. 'Comrade, will you have some tea?'

'No,' said M.K.

They sat in silence for some time. Then Shunya started the conversation.

'Madhavan Kutty Nair, Marx-worshipper, what brings you here to the Void? Do I look like an animal in the zoo? Go hasten your revolution. Some of your legislators are drinking the blood of the proletariat. Don't bother me.'

M.K. spoke in an even tone, trying to hide his anger and surprise, 'All sadhus are frauds, parasites who live by cheating the credulous. I came here partly out of curiosity, but I also appreciate the advice and support you gave Meenakshi, my niece. Frankly, I think you are a crazy fellow and foolish, too. If certain people were to know you were behind this marriage, they will kill you. And how come you know about Marx? You must be an educated man.'

'I am the Void, Shunya. Do you understand? I am nothing. One day I shall rest six feet below the earth's surface, and so will you. But you probably don't think about it. You have studied dialectical materialism, but have you ever questioned it? Question everything. Theories, theories, all kinds of theories. Go have some toddy. Wash out all the theories and live in peace.'

'Saami,' M.K. said, 'I won't argue with you. You are different from what I had expected. Maybe you are mad, but there is, as they say, a method in your madness, and you seem to be an educated lunatic. One last question. Some people say that your blessings bring good luck. Do you believe this yourself?'

'People can say what they want. I am nothing and nobody. I am the Void. I need nothing, nothing at all. All I need is a little bit of bull-shit or cow dung to plaster the floor of my dwelling place. Aha! From your expression I see that you don't like bull-shit, but my dear fellow, bull-shit has been used in this country for many things. As fuel, for plastering the walls and floors of mud huts, and even as medicine. Ask the great Ayurvedic Vaidyas. Panchagavya contains cow shit, cow pee, cow's milk, ghee and curd. Well, you don't have to take it if you don't want to; it doesn't matter, but tell me, why have you given up playing the flute for so long? Start again. Music is food for the soul. Your soul is hungry. I can see that.'

'But Saami,' said M.K., trying hard to keep his voice calm and unaffected by the shocking discovery that this seemingly crazy fakir seemed to know facts about his life which he had till then thought were known only to a few. 'Who told you about the flute? Couldn't be Meena because she doesn't know herself; even her mother doesn't. That was long ago when I fell in love...but how do you know?'

'Ha, ha,' laughed Shunya, 'don't ask me how, okay, but start playing your flute again. Bring some music into your life, man. Go and fill your soul with ragas.'

M.K. walked away without a word. Shunya retired to his hut. Nobody had ever entered the hut after he had begun to reside there, and no one knew what he did inside.

8

That night, shortly after M.K.'s departure, three men met secretly in an isolated coconut grove not far from the toddy shop. They were Ouseph, Jabbar the butcher, and Shankunni. Jabbar, who was Salim's uncle, was seething with rage because Salim had run away with a Hindu girl, an infidel, instead of marrying his daughter Shirin. On the other hand, Shankunni thought it was outrageous that a good Hindu girl had eloped with a Muslim 'barbarian'.

The meeting had been called to work out a strategy to deal with their common enemy: Shunya. He was certainly a danger to the established order, a cancerous growth which had to be excised before it turned unmanageable.

'We need to do something about this Saami,' said Jabbar, opening the conversation. 'I hear he stood behind Meenakshi and Salim, and encouraged them to break all conventions. Without his support, they wouldn't have dared to get married. We can't let this go on.'

'I was thinking the same,' said Ouseph, turning up the wick of the hurricane lamp to make it a shade brighter.

'We must teach him a lesson,' said Shankunni, 'otherwise all our youngsters will be corrupted. They'll become rebels. I feel he is a Marxist in disguise. Comrade M.K. went to see him. Marxists are godless, religion-less, casteless. We have to do something.'

'You are right,' said Ouseph, 'Marxist or not, we must do something about him. Salim's father has been silenced. Our youngsters cannot be allowed to defy their religious heads, and such marriages cannot be allowed to go unchallenged. No, no, this cannot be. If we teach this Shunya a lesson, everyone will get the message.'

'We have to do it quickly,' said Shankunni, 'before he turns into a cult figure. He is already regarded by some as an Avadhuta, an enlightened holy man. But what should we do and how?'

'If you ask me,' said Ouseph still seething with anger, 'the best thing to do to a man who corrupts the youth is to finish him off. Kill him. No one is going to find out. Go to the hut in the middle of the night, soak the thatched roof and walls with petrol, and set it on fire. Such accidents do happen, don't they?'

Shankunni and Jabbar were in complete agreement.

'It's probably best if we hire somebody to do the job,' said Jabbar, 'I know the right person, Kunjappan, the washerman. He has become an alcoholic. He has given up washing clothes and starts drinking from the morning. He is also always short of cash. The other day, he accosted me and said, "Jabbar-ikka, I'll do anything you want me to, just give me twenty-five rupees. I cannot live without drinking."'

'No,' interjected Shankunni. 'What if he refuses and spreads the word?'

Ouseph agreed. He said, 'No one else should get to know anything about this. We'll have to do it ourselves.'

Three days later, on a dark, moonless night at 2.30 a.m., the three men, armed with cans of petrol, matchboxes and a flashlight, crept stealthily towards the hut where Shunya lived. No one saw them, or so they thought, except the big horned owl which was sitting on the longest branch of the jackfruit tree. The owl hooted thrice in an almost human voice.

'What's that?' whispered Shankunni, fear causing his hair to stand on end.

'Nothing, it's just an owl,' whispered Ouseph.

'It sounded so human,' said Jabbar. 'Let's start quickly. I can hear a steady snore from inside. Let's finish the job before he wakes up. Shankunni, secure the bolt outside the door firmly.'

Shankunni bolted the door from outside using the rusty, old-fashioned bolt, trying to be as noiseless as possible. The small window at the back of the hut was open but no one could escape through it since it had a strong iron grille fixed to the wooden frame. Shankunni peeped in. It was utterly dark inside. He too thought he'd heard Shunya snore.

They had come well prepared. Ouseph fixed the small bamboo ladder to the wall and held it. Jabbar climbed up and doused the thatched roof with petrol. Then he climbed down, and together they threw petrol on the walls and the door. For good measure, they poured some into the hut through the window.

Ouseph struck the matches and threw them one after another on the roof and the walls of the hut. He threw some into the hut as well. In no time, angry tongues of fire engulfed the hut. They also threw the bamboo ladder into the fire and fled from the scene.

Finding their way with the help of the flashlight, they reached the safety of the dilapidated temple not far away from the hut. There, huddled under the old peepal tree, they watched the hut burn down.

Someone in the neighbourhood woke up, saw the fire, and alerted the public. Soon, people could be seen shouting and running, carrying buckets of water to douse the fire, but it was too late. Before they could put it out, the hut was by and large gutted.

'Done,' said Jabbar, 'I think the fellow didn't even have time to wake up. Burnt to ashes, I am sure.'

The branch of the jackfruit tree on which the horned owl habitually perched was also destroyed by the fire. It now sat on the peepal tree near the dilapidated temple in which they were hiding, and hooted again. 'Blasted owl,' said Shankunni, shivering, 'it seems to be hiding somewhere above our heads. Wish we had killed it too.'

'Don't worry, Shankunni,' said Ouseph, 'owls cannot speak.'

'But this nut can,' said a strange voice from the top of the tree.

'Who's that?' they screamed in unison, trembling with fear. The hidden voice chuckled, sending shivers up their spine.

'I knew you would come for me, wise men. I am Shunya! Zero! Nobody! Just as I am sitting now on the peepal tree, I was sitting on the top of the coconut tree while you hatched the plot, and heard everything. Ha! So you thought I was burnt to ashes? You can't kill me. I am a ghost. I am the Void.' With that, Shunya jumped down from the tree and stood before them.

It took them a few seconds to react. They ran as fast as they could and disappeared into the darkness. 'Don't worry,' Shunya shouted after them, 'I won't tell anybody. Have no fear.'

9

By the time the fire died down, it was dawn. Hardly anything was left of the hut. Part of the jackfruit tree had been burnt, but the toddy shop remained untouched. The police had arrived and so had Sadasivan and his wife. While Sadasivan, the policemen and other members of the public searched for Shunya's body among the still smouldering remains, Sadasivan's wife, Bhavani, sat under the slightly burnt jackfruit tree, sobbing uncontrollably.

'Bhavani, silly girl, why are you sobbing?' said a familiar voice.

Bhavani looked up and cried out, 'Saami!' Sadasivan heard her and turned around. He saw Shunya standing there, holding the bamboo flute in his left hand, and trying hard with his right to prevent Bhavani from falling at his feet.

'There he is! Saami is alive,' shouted Sadasivan, and bounded towards him. Soon, a crowd which included the policemen, gathered around Shunya.

'Somebody set fire to the hut,' said Shunya, 'some fools. But can you burn Zero? It is nothing. They thought they heard me snore. Sheer imagination, a mere fantasy. Sadasiva, may I sleep in the toddy shop till you do up the cottage? What do you think?'

'Yes, Saami, whatever you say. You have blessed my life. You are divine. You are not an ordinary human being. I'll rebuild the hut soon. I will make it better than before. Don't go anywhere, Saami, please.'

The sub-inspector of police, Chandu, addressed Shunya, 'Shunyam or Saami or whatever you are called,' he said mockingly, 'did you see the culprits? Can you identify them? Or did you set fire to the hut yourself?'

'Stupid ass, mairae,' said Shunya, 'I saw nobody. Why should I see anybody? No body, only mind. Understood? You won't understand.'

'If you abuse me,' said the policeman, trembling with anger and moving closer to Shunya, 'I'll break your balls and lock you up.'

M.K. Nair, Meenakshi's uncle, had appeared unexpectedly at the scene. He made his way through the little crowd that had gathered and faced the inspector.

'Inspector saar,' he said sternly, 'cool down. He's not normal, don't you see? I think you better go home and rest. You must be exhausted.'

'If you say so,' said the Inspector, 'but I'll continue my investigation. If you hadn't intervened, Nair saar, I would have broken his…okay. See you later.'

He turned on his heels and walked away. The small posse of policemen followed him.

'I am not normal, yeah?' laughed Shunya, 'In the Englishman's language, I would be called a nut. Coconut, groundnut, betelnut, what nut? Nut-nut. Ha!'

M.K. said, 'You seem to be a well-educated man. I am curious. Who are you?'

'Who are you? Great question! Great thinkers haven't found an answer to this question. Who are you? I know the answer: zero, shunya, nothingness.

'Some years ago, a nondescript half-naked man, living in the Arunachala hills in South India, asked the same question in a different way. Who am I? The body is mine, the mind is mine, the brain is mine, so who on earth am I? I say, Shunya, nothingness.'

'I will discuss this with you some other time, Saami,' said M.K. 'When shall I come?'

'Any time, oh devotee of Marx. May his flowing beard save you from nothingness. It's frightening—annihilation! Go read your bible, Das Kapital, or better still, get back to your music. Play the flute.'

M.K. said impulsively, 'Saami, I notice that you have a flute. What if I said, "I shall resume my music if you give me your flute." Would you give it to me then?'

'All at the right time, not now. Go now, comrade.'

☙

As M.K. left, Sadasivan thanked him. He said, 'Nair saar, if you hadn't intervened, I would have had to protect Saami with all my strength from the policeman, and ended up in the police lock-up myself. Thank you so much. Do come and meet Saami sometime.'

'I will. If you need any help, let me know.'

10

For a month from the night of the fire, Shunya slept in a corner of the toddy shop at night, and spent the rest of the day sitting under the jackfruit tree, watching the masons and the carpenters build a single-roomed cottage for him, which was to have a tiled roof and red cement floor.

Since the day his old abode was burnt down, he had discarded his upper garment, the white cotton shirt. He wore just the single piece of cloth, the mundu, around his waist.

Myriad stories, each more fantastic than the other, which made the rounds after that eventful night, had made him a celebrity of sorts. More and more people came to see him.

In one version of the event, an eyewitness swore to have seen Shunya fly out of the burning house like a shooting star, land in front of Bhavani, and revert to his real shape. Another reported to have seen him ascend bodily from the fire, complete with a halo, and descend again in a physical body. 'Why not?' said the narrator, 'Jesus was resurrected.' Yet another version made him out to be indestructible, and painted a glorious picture of him walking out of the fire, unscathed, not a single hair burnt.

The perpetrators of the crime added their own spice to the stories, as a kind of thanksgiving for not reporting them to the police.

A few non-believers said he had escaped through sheer luck. The local tantrik, who was beginning to get jealous of Shunya, tried to spread the rumour that Shunya had probably set the cottage on fire himself, but he was silenced by the majority who believed in Shunya's powers.

People thronged to Sadasivan's toddy shop to have a glimpse of or perhaps be touched or blessed by Shunya. Some came out of mere curiosity.

Sadasivan worried that his Saami might get fed up of the crowds and run away. But Shunya seemed unperturbed and continued to drink his black tea and chat with the visitors, sometimes engaging in serious dialogue and, at other times, showering them with the vilest abuse.

However, Sadasivan did work out a kind of schedule. No outsider was allowed to disturb Shunya till seven in the evening. A six-foot-high bamboo screen barrier was erected around the backyard for this purpose. At nine, all visitors were gently asked to leave.

Soon, the new cottage was ready. Shunya moved into it one night at ten. Sadasivan led him to the cottage, placed a clay pot filled with drinking water in one corner, unrolled a brown straw mat and asked, 'What else do you need, Saami?'

'Nothing,' said Shunya, placing his bundle of dirty clothes and his flute in the corner of the room. 'You may go now.'

Just then, there came the sound of a dog howling not too far away.

'Ah! He has come,' said Shunya and stepped out of the cottage. Sadasivan followed him and saw a big, well-built mongrel, jet black in colour, standing near the jackfruit tree, his right paw held up.

'Come, my friend, come,' said Shunya. The dog limped towards him, whimpering in pain.

Shunya kneeled down beside the dog and patted him with great affection. 'He is Ponnu', he said, 'real gold. Sadasiva, bring me some toddy and a small bowl.' Sadasivan went to the bar and returned in minutes with a clay bowl and a bottle of toddy. Shunya poured some of the toddy into the bowl and spoke to the dog, 'Ponnu, drink my friend, drink. It will relieve you of the pain. It is a minor injury. You'll get over it soon.'

The dog stopped whimpering and drank the toddy with quick slurps. Shunya poured some toddy on the dog's injured paw. It yelped once and then quietened down. When the bowl was empty, Shunya poured whatever remained in the bottle into it and said, 'Finish it up, old boy.'

The dog licked the bowl clean and looked up at Shunya. 'You drunk,' Shunya said, laughing loudly, 'brother Sadasivan here will give you some food and toddy every day. Won't you, Sadasiva?'

'Yes, Saami.' Sadasivan nodded.

'Ponnu, you can leave early in the morning and come back at nine at night. Then you can drink your toddy, eat your food, and sleep under the jackfruit tree. If you need to see Shunya, bark twice, understand?'

The dog nodded.

'Are you hungry now?'

The dog shook its head.

'All right, then go to sleep and go away just before dawn and come back in the night.'

The dog lay down under the jackfruit tree and instantly fell asleep.

'Sadasiva,' said Shunya looking up at the sky, 'the rains are sure to come soon. Won't Ponnu be drenched in the rain?'

'Yes, Saami.'

'So what do we do?'

'I can build a small kennel for him in no time,' said Sadasivan, 'but then what happens to the congregation when it rains? I have been thinking about it lately. More and more people are coming to see you. They certainly can't use the toddy shop. So it would be a good idea to make a thatched roof to cover the whole courtyard.'

'That will cost you a lot of money.'

'No, not much, Saami. We'll do it ourselves and save labour. Coconut leaf thatch is available in plenty these days, because most people make tiled roofs for their houses. All we need to procure is bamboo. That I can get from Panicker without much difficulty. If you agree, I'll start the work and finish it before the monsoon starts.'

'Do it,' said Shunya and walking into the cottage, shutting the door behind him.

In ten days, a thatched roof supported by strong bamboo posts came up, covering the entire courtyard.

Shambu, an expert thatcher, boasted about the special technique he had adopted to thatch the roof so that the trunk of the jackfruit tree could pass through a hole in the roof. It was built with such precision and waterproofed so well that 'not a single drop of water could trickle down through it.'

Ponnu, the black dog, slept under the jackfruit tree every night. Sadasivan personally gave him his bowl of toddy and fed him before locking up the bar and going home. On Monday nights, when the bar was closed, he would bring Ponnu's food along with Shunya's meal.

At times, Shunya would come out of the cottage, stroke Ponnu's head and talk to him. Every morning, much before dawn, he would run out and disappear.

Soon, the monsoon came and, as usual, it rained incessantly for days. Instead of cats and dogs, it rained frogs and toads and innumerable flying insects. The croaking of the courting frogs filled the air. The temple pond was full once again. The trees and plants celebrated wordlessly. There was water everywhere. Children played joyously in the puddles, not caring for the cold and fever that would follow. Shunya loved the rains too and, at times, went out to play with the children. He often sat in the now covered courtyard and watched the rain, laughing and shouting, 'Come wash away the dirt, Lord of the Rains, haha!'

Ponnu stuck to his routine even during the monsoons. No one knew where he went during the day but he appeared every night in the courtyard beside the jackfruit tree, sometimes without a drop of water on his body, and sometimes fully drenched by the rain.

One rainy night, after he had closed the bar, Sadasivan went to the courtyard to feed Ponnu. Ponnu was lying close to Shunya's cottage licking his wet paws. Sadasivan first poured the toddy into the bowl and waited for him to finish. Ponnu lapped up the toddy with great gusto.

'Drink quickly, Ponnu,' said Sadasivan, 'I'll have to give you your food and hurry back home.'

'Be patient, Sadasiva,' said a voice. It was so similar to Shunya's that Sadasivan turned in the direction of the cottage, expecting to see his beloved Saami's face, but there was no one there. The door was shut. Then the voice said, 'I am talking to you here, and you are looking there.'

This time, Sadasivan's hair stood on end, for he realised that it was the black dog, Ponnu, who was speaking.

'All right, give me the food now and wait for a while; I have to talk to you.'

With trembling hands, Sadasivan pushed the mutton curry and rice from the steel container into Ponnu's clay bowl, and stood there waiting respectfully.

'Sit down,' said Ponnu and proceeded to lick the bowl clean. Sadasivan sat down close by.

After finishing his food, Ponnu said, 'Water, water.'

Sadasivan poured water into the bowl and sat down again.

The croaking of the frogs suddenly rose to a crescendo. Ponnu licked his lips, sat up on his haunches facing Sadasivan, and said, 'Manduks, the frogs, are chanting the Mandukya Upanishad, the wisdom of the ancients, and here I am, a dog teaching man.

'Listen, Sadasiva, this world is a mirage, a bubble that can burst anytime. Understand this and be free of all expectations. Happiness is a state of mind not dependent on anything you possess. The fakir with no possessions sitting under the tree is often happier than the man who owns a fleet of Mercedes and BMWs.'

'All that may be true,' said Sadasivan, recovering his composure somewhat, 'but tell me, who are you?'

'Aha! What a wise question. I am a black dog; Shunya calls me gold, Ponnu. I am his friend and I love to be where he is, but only in the night. I won't tell you where I am during the day and no one can find out. I am not an ordinary dog, you see.'

'Then?'

'Now look,' said Ponnu and before Sadasivan's astonished eyes, he levitated and rose to the level of the roof. Then he descended back to his original position on the ground. 'What say you?'

'Wonderful, great,' said Sadasivan rubbing his eyes and

wondering if he was actually awake or dreaming. 'How did you do that?'

'Questions, questions, questions,' said Ponnu in an exasperated tone, 'that's all that you human beings do—ask questions. You'll get no answers because the questions are all wrong. Anyway, keep all the happenings of today to yourself. You may reveal them to Thambi when I am gone.'

'Who's Thambi?' asked Sadasivan.

'He is yet to come but he will. Now, that's enough. Not a word to anyone, remember? The food was great and so was the toddy. Go now.'

From inside the cottage, Shunya shouted, 'Will you two shut up now?'

'Sorry, Shunya, I am going to sleep now,' said Ponnu and leaning his body against the wall of the cottage, he closed his eyes and fell asleep.

Sadasivan walked out of the courtyard, got into his Fiat, and drove away. No one except him got to know that Ponnu, the black dog, was different from other dogs. 'In any case,' he said to himself, 'anyone I say this to would conclude that either I have gone crazy or have started drinking too much.'

Many months later, after Ponnu had vanished, Sadasivan related the strange experience of that rainy night to Thambi, who had arrived just as Ponnu had predicted. Shunya never mentioned the incident and Sadasivan never asked him about it.

Raghavan, Sadasivan's assistant, said that once he secretly followed Ponnu when he ran out of his night's resting place, well before dawn. Nobody except Sadasivan believed what Raghavan said, for it was common knowledge that Raghavan was a ganja addict. He said, 'The black dog ran fast and soon started flying like a bird. He flew and disappeared over the hill.'

But after the day he said he saw the dog fly, Raghavan was never again the same person. He insisted on going every night to see Ponnu and prostrate himself before him. Soon, he developed the habit of bowing down to all the dogs in the neighbourhood. He was nicknamed Patti Raghavan, meaning 'Dog Raghavan'.

11

A month after Ponnu's arrival came Thambi. An educated young man from Suchindram in the neighbouring state of Tamil Nadu, he came upon Shunya while wandering in search of a spiritual guide. His real name was Kumar, and it was Shunya who named him Thambi, which means 'younger brother'.

After Thambi came Bob Hawkins, a professor of religion and philosophy at a renowned university in California. Shunya was now becoming well-known, and many more visitors began to arrive.

Kumar, who later became Shunya's constant companion, was to play an important part in the drama that was to unfold. He was named after the spear-wielding, handsome, high-flying young god, Srikumar, who had two consorts, and always travelled by air, seated on a celestial peacock. According to the Hindu pantheon, he was the son of Shiva and Parvati, and the brother of the elephant-headed god Ganesh, whose vehicle was the lowly mouse.

Kumar himself was quite good-looking. He was dark-complexioned, with large and thoughtful eyes, a modest nose, full lips, and a neatly trimmed black beard which, together with his glistening, black, flowing locks gathered into a ponytail, gave him a distinctly 'arty' appearance. He was slim and of medium height.

His parents came from an orthodox Brahmin family hailing from the temple town of Suchindram in the Kanyakumari district. For many generations, he and his wife's ancestors had been officiating priests in the main and subsidiary shrines of the locality.

Kumar's father, Kuppuswamy Iyer, was the first in the family to have taken up secular studies. He had studied at the American College at Madurai on a scholarship, and had graduated in mathematics. After returning to his native village, he had married Kamala, who hailed from a nearby Brahmin settlement, and found a job as a mathematics teacher at the local high school.

The reason he had decided to not seek his fortune in big cities like Madras or Bombay was his deep sense of duty to his parents. They refused to leave the village. He was their only child, the only son, and his parents were old and infirm. He considered looking after them his sacred duty. Fortunately for him, Kamala treated them like her own and satisfied their smallest whim.

When it came to Kumar's future, Kuppuswami Iyer did his best to ensure that he received a good education that prepared him for a brilliant career. 'Though you are our only child, do not worry about us,' he often told his son. 'Go where you want and do the best you can. I want you to make up for what I have missed, and your mother thinks so, too.'

Kumar didn't disappoint them. He did even better than what they had imagined. After being a topper in his high school and intermediate levels, he was admitted to the Regional Engineering College at Chennai. He graduated with distinction, and went to the US to do his master's at the Massachusetts Institute of Technology. He landed a job as a research assistant at the same university as soon as he graduated.

At twenty-six, he was enjoying his new-found freedom, position and status when he had to go back to his village on a short leave, summoned by his father who wanted to finalise his marriage to Shyamala, Kumar's maternal uncle's daughter. Although he was in no great hurry to get married, Kumar dared not disagree with his parents and show disrespect. Shyamala was eighteen years old at the time.

Kumar liked what he saw. Since he had last met her, she had matured from a wide-eyed, untidy and shy child into a pretty and coy damsel with long black tresses. He almost fell in love.

The engagement was formalised by a simple ceremony. All the villagers were invited. Kumar went back to Massachusetts. He was to return the following year and get married.

'Hey there,' said Shyamala as he was leaving, her body well-hidden behind the big banana tree near the gate with only her face showing, 'write to me, okay, in English. I can read slowly. My English will improve with reading. I…I….no, nothing. See you.' She ran back into the house, her anklets jingling.

'Watch out,' shouted Kumar, as he went out of the gate, accompanied by his father and uncle who were going with him to the bus-stop, 'you are getting too American these days.' Everyone laughed.

As Kumar sat in the bus which would take him to Thiruvananthapuram, from where he would catch a train to Bombay and fly to the US, he thought of what he was going to write in his first letter to Shyamala.

But the first letter was never written. From the day he set his eyes on Leena, the beautiful, blonde American research assistant with the red, juicy lips and green eyes, who had been newly appointed to coordinate with him on his project, everything and everybody, including Shyamala, were forgotten. Leena Smith, the American typhoon, swept him off his feet. They went to the movies together, ate together, shopped together, and it seemed that they were in love, or so thought Kumar after he had been initiated by Leena into the orgasmic mysteries of sexual union.

But, in less than a year, the typhoon had moved off in another direction. One fateful evening, Kumar came upon Leena in the laboratory passionately making love to the tall and well-built Professor Herzberger, their guide. He found himself dumped, low, limp, and dry. The thoughts of Leena's warm and wet insides, and the inebriating taste of her bright red, fruit-flavoured lipstick, became mere memories. Bitterness and depression set in. But worse things were to follow.

Dazzled by the golden blonde strands which had captured his imagination like a noose, he'd turned a cold shoulder to the coal-haired Shyamala and had, only some weeks earlier, informed both their parents that the engagement was off. He would never marry an illiterate village lass he'd thought. Golden opportunities awaited him in the land of plenty, whose privileged portals he could enter effortlessly leaning on Leena.

Shyamala, her dreams shattered, jumped into the village pond and ended her life. Unable to bear the shame and sorrow, Shyamala's father and mother swallowed kill-bug, a lethal insecticide, and died one after another.

This was followed by the death of Kumar's father. He had suffered a heart-attack, which happened ten minutes after he had written a strongly worded letter to his son saying that he never wanted to see him again, ever. Only Kumar's mother now remained.

All this information burst upon Kumar like a bombshell

when his paternal cousin, Ganesh, with great effort, managed to get through to him on the telephone. 'Your father's cremation will take place this evening. The village elders are not agreeing to wait for you. They say it will take you a few days to reach here. The body shouldn't be kept for so long. I have been asked to officiate in your place. Come as quickly as you can, Kumar,' he said. 'Your mother has almost gone mad with grief and is crying for you all the time. See her before she, too, passes away. She refuses to eat or drink and keeps saying, "My Kumar will come." Forget everything else and come if you want to see her alive.'

The world turned upside-down for Kumar. He found himself marooned in a strange land. There was no one he could call his own, no one except his mother, who was so far away. Who cared for him? Nobody! Nothing mattered now, except to be near his mother who had suckled him on her lap.

He didn't even bother to apply for leave. He went to the travel agent and made arrangements directly.

One hot afternoon, four days later, travel-worn, jet-lagged, grief-stricken and weary, Kumar alighted from a bus at Suchindram Main Bus Stand, carrying just a blue backpack. His mind was still in a state of shock and somewhat disoriented.

In fifteen minutes, he was in the agraharam, the Brahmin quarter of the village. On the way he met a couple of people who averted their eyes and refused to speak, except for their old faithful servant Baalu. '*Chinaiyya!*' he exclaimed and began to cry, beating his forehead with his hands.

'Baalu, where is Ganesh?'

'Went to Tirunelvelli, young master,' he said between sobs, 'Your mother is in the house.'

As Kumar walked towards the familiar white-washed and tiled house, one of his distant aunts came out, took a look at him, frowned, and walked out muttering angrily under her breath, 'Only she is left now, waiting to die. Go and send her off, too.'

Kumar went in, crossed the verandah, and entered the inner courtyard. His mother was sitting in the old cane armchair, right under the framed photograph of her late husband, his father, her head tonsured, and clad in the white robes of a widow.

'Amma,' Kumar called softly, tears blurring his eyes, 'It's me, Kumar, Amma. Your accursed son.'

'Kumara?' she said, 'No, no, that can't be. My Kumara is in America, but he'll come. He can't stay away from me.'

'I am Kumara, Amma. I have come.'

'Come closer, let me see,' she said, trying to stand up with difficulty.

Kumar ran towards her and fell at her feet. She bent down, lifted his head and placed it in her lap. 'It's you, Kumara, Kumara, I...' she wept uncontrollably. They wept together for a long time, holding each other.

Recovering somewhat, she wiped his face dry and said, 'Your Appa is gone and you know...'

'Amma, I know. Ganesh wrote to me. Now I'll look after you.'

'No, no. You go back and live happily.'

'No, Amma, I am not going back. I came, even though I'm late, to look after you.'

'Okay, we'll talk about that later. I'll call Bhanu. She has been looking after me. You must be tired and hungry. I'll ask her to cook your favourite tomato rasam and puliyodharai rice.'

'No, Amma, I don't think she'll come. I'll cook for you today. Remember how well I used to cook? Meanwhile, why don't you sleep for a while?'

He led her to the bedroom, and stroked her forehead until she fell asleep holding his hand. Carefully, he extricated his fingers and walked to the verandah. Baalu was waiting for him.

Kumar gave him some money and sent him to the market to get provisions. Then he went to the well, and drew out a bucket of clear, cold water, and had a bath outdoors. Towelling himself dry, he went to the little shrine room where all the statuettes and pictures of gods and their ancestors were kept. He bowed down and felt great revulsion for the silent, smiling gods, who seemed to be uncaring while humans wept in misery. He sprang out of the room and went to sit on the verandah.

His thoughts went back to Shyamala, innocent wide-eyed Shyamala, whom he had betrayed. If only she hadn't ended her life. He thought of her parents, his late uncle and aunt who had been so fond of him. How many times had Shyamala and he, as little children, sat in the kitchen and eaten the delicious idli and sambar that his aunt had made. Tears rolled down his eyes.

A barefooted, matted-haired and heavily bearded man walked in from the gate. He was wearing just a small, ochre-coloured towel that barely covered his nakedness.

Seeing Kumar, he walked towards him. Kumar stood up wiping his tears. Without a word, the stranger handed him a dirty piece of paper with something scribbled on it in Tamil. 'Who…,' Kumar started saying, but the stranger just turned and walked away.

'Wait,' called out Kumar after him, but the stranger

had vanished. Kumar, too tired to go after him, sat down on the bench and tried to read what was written. It was a poem:

Life is so fleeting, you fool,
Who knows when death will strike?
Everything comes and goes,
And so do you, if you follow the rules.
Break all rules,
Swim in the joy of consciousness,
Be free.
Find the true guide,
Dump all becoming,
And in nothingness, just be, be free.

It was signed: Shunya—the Nothing. Kumar read it carefully a few times and then, on an impulse, tucked it safely in his rucksack. For the next three days, whenever he found a little time in the midst of all the hard work involved in looking after his mother, cooking for her, bathing her, talking to her and so on, he read the note with care and often wondered who the mysterious stranger was.

On the fourth day, his mother passed away peacefully in her sleep sometime before dawn with her head in his lap. Kumar was surprised at how matter-of-factly he had accepted the death of his dear mother.

He broke a few rules. He didn't cry, he did not even wait for the funeral. He gently covered her face with a white sheet and went to the kitchen. He took an old cloth shoulder-bag of the kind carried by villagers, and packed a towel, two white mundus, a notepad and a pencil, some money and, of course, the paper which the stranger had given to him. Then he walked out of the house and the village before it woke up.

Wearing rubber slippers, with the bag in one hand and an aluminium water pot in the other, dressed in a simple mundu, with a faded white towel thrown across his shoulders, he looked the quintessential wandering sadhu, a seeker of truth. In Massachusetts, they would have called him a hippy.

❧

His destination was Kanyakumari, India's land's end in the south, where the waters of the Indian Ocean, the Arabian Sea and the Bay of Bengal intermingled. His aim was to find a spiritual teacher. He covered the first four kilometres on foot, and the rest of the sixteen kilometres by a local bus.

He reached Kanyakumari just in time to see the golden sun in all its glory rise up from the horizon, bathing the sky with varied hues. He sat on a rock on the sea shore and forgot everything for a while. When his thoughts returned, he made his way to the temple of the Virgin Goddess, which he had visited many times before as a young boy. The diamond on her nose ring shone brightly.

Legend has it that at one time the diamond shone so brightly that ships sailing in the night located the shore by its light. The belief that the goddess would punish them discouraged thieves from trying to steal it.

Kumar bought himself some tea from a beachside tea shop and walked towards the water. Sitting on the sand with his feet in the water, he watched the waves crashing against the large boulder about a kilometre from the shore.

It was called the Vivekananda Rock. The well-known monk, Swami Vivekananda, who had taken India's spiritual teachings to the West in the early twentieth century, had meditated on it for three full days.

His father had been fond of Vivekananda's books and Kumar had read some of them as a young man, only to be discarded later in favour of Einstein and Russell. Now, parts of what he had read came back to him in bits and pieces. Suddenly, he felt the urgent need to solve the mystery of existence. He took out the bit of paper which had become sacred to him, and unfolding it carefully, read it again.

One sentence seemed to stand out clearer than the rest: *Find the true guide.* But where was he? Or she? Perhaps in the snow-clad Himalayan mountains. In any case, he couldn't afford to live in Kanyakumari for long. It was too close to Suchindram. Someone would find him, and he wanted to have nothing to do with his past.

On one of the numerous boulders scattered on the sea shore, not far from where he was, sat a venerable old, shaven-headed and saffron-robed renunciant. Perhaps he could help Kumar.

Kumar approached the sadhu. He turned out to be very friendly. Yes, he had travelled extensively in the Himalayas. The mountains were beautiful, and so was the great river Ganga, and so on and so forth, but there was no guarantee of finding a true spiritual master even there. Most of the ashrams had become commercial ventures. Gurus catered to rich foreigners and worshipped dollars more than the gods. Some had their own private airplanes and boasted of air-conditioned caves. There were also the hemp-smokers who revelled in their hallucinations. All places of pilgrimage were bursting with tourists and in this set-up, it was almost impossible to find a genuine sage.

But then, great sages were not restricted to the Himalayas. They could be anywhere, and if you were a serious seeker, you would surely find a true sage.

The sadhu had himself had the good fortune of sitting at the feet of one such sage in the south, the great Ramana, who lived in Tiruvannamalai. Unfortunately, he had passed away long ago.

'Can you be my guide?' Kumar asked him.

'No, I am still far from my goal.'

'Then what shall I do?'

'I haven't met this man, because I no longer seek a guide, having accepted Ramana as my master,' said the sadhu, 'but I heard that a strange and eccentric sage lives in a place called Tirumala, in the suburbs near Thiruvananthapuram, the capital of Kerala. He is called Shunya Saami. My brother comes from those parts and he wrote to me about him. So far he is known only among a small circle. Perhaps it is worth a try. Thiruvananthapuram is not so far away and who knows?

'But let me warn you. Some of these chaps are quite bizarre. So be on your guard and be patient.'

Kumar thanked him, and within minutes, he was on a bus bound for Thiruvananthapuram.

12

O n alighting he made enquiries and located Shunya's abode without much difficulty. He was surprised that a sage should live in the backyard of a toddy shop. The time was 1 p.m. Sadasivan, the owner of the toddy shop, told him that he would have to wait till 7 p.m. to meet Shunya.

Notwithstanding his ferocious moustache and boxer-like body, Kumar found Sadasivan to be a gentle, friendly guy. He explained to Kumar that on account of more and more people coming to see Saami, he had devised what he called a 'general satsang' twice a week on Tuesday and Friday, when a number of people were allowed to gather in front of his cottage and interact with him.

At 7 p.m., after his only meal of the day, Shunya would come out of his cottage and sit with the public for two hours. People were free to ask questions or seek his help. But they were not allowed to touch his feet, a rule that had been put in place for their own safety. 'People who have tried to touch his feet have been badly rebuked by Saami,' said Sadasivan.

Anyone who wanted to meet Shunya alone had to present themselves at these gatherings and ask for a private interview. If Shunya decided that they could see him in private, they would be asked to come back on any other day of the week except Monday. Monday was the day of rest. Even the toddy shop was closed.

It happened to be a Friday, so Sadasivan told Kumar that he could wait for the general satsang.

'You can eat some rice and fish curry or some rice and sambar, and wait. If you want to rest, you can sleep on the verandah after having your food. What's your name?'

'Kumar.'

Kumar looked around the toddy shop. A few men sat drinking toddy. From the way they talked and laughed, he knew that many of them were drunk. Once again, the thought occurred to him that this was indeed a strange habitat for a holy man. 'Yes, I'll have some rice and sambar. I am a vegetarian,' he said, and found himself a quiet bench in the corner.

'What about some toddy?'

'No, I don't drink.'

'Oh! Ok.'

Kumar was surprised to hear this, but decided to wait and see things for himself.

Hunger increased the taste of the simple food. After the meal, he felt tired and drowsy. Sadasivan led him to the verandah and spread a mat and gave him a pillow. 'I'll call you before seven,' he said, 'you seem quite young and, if I am not mistaken, educated too. Now sleep.'

Kumar merely smiled and laid his head on the pillow. The last thought that flashed through his mind before he fell into a deep slumber was, 'What kind of a sadhu would he be? He lives in a toddy shop.'

At ten minutes to seven, Sadasivan woke him up from a beautiful dream in which he had been flying high above the clouds, seated on an indigo-hued swan.

Kumar splashed water on his face and patted it dry with a towel before he was led to the covered courtyard on which stood the cottage, beside the jackfruit tree. About twenty-five people, men and women, young and old, sat on straw mats spread on the floor paved with rough granite slabs. A placard was stuck on one side of the bamboo-mat enclosure. It was in Malayalam, a language which, like most inhabitants of the neighbouring state of Tamil Nadu, he could speak reasonably well but could not read.

'The notice says,' whispered Sadasivan, 'do not touch Saami's feet. He doesn't like it.' Kumar sat down in the last row.

Shunya's entry was quite dramatic. All of a sudden, the door of the cottage flung open and out sprang a thin man of medium height, wearing only a white mundu wrapped around his waist. His long, greying hair was gathered into a bun on the crown of his head. His brown face with the sparse, drooping moustache, the thin, pointed beard, and narrow, slanting eyes made him look like the picture of a Zen master that Kumar had seen on the cover of a book in a bookstore in New York City.

The most striking feature of the man, however, was his sharp, darting eyes, which seemed to be looking for someone or something. For a second, as they came to rest on Kumar's face, he felt as if his brain was being examined in depth, every neuron x-rayed.

Shunya then leapt towards the jackfruit tree, and sat cross-legged under it in the Buddha posture. Then he rubbed his hands together vigorously and laughed loudly, and in the most un-Buddha-like manner, shouted, 'Shit, shit, shit!' Kumar wondered if he was sitting before a holy man or a madman.

Looking around at the people sitting in front of him, he said, 'Why have you all come? Umph! I am Shunya, nothing! I can give you nothing, you will receive nothing. Who can give anything? Waste of time, waste of time. No time, no time, nothing to waste.'

Sadasivan, who remained standing, said softly, 'They have all come to have your darshan, Saami. Please bless them.'

'You,' he shouted at Sadasivan, 'you don't tell me what to do. Tap toddy, tap all the time till the nectar flows, tuk, tuk tuk. Go get me some black tea.'

'Here, Saami,' said Sadasivan, gesturing towards the kettle and the glass placed on the ground. 'I have brought it for you already.'

'Aah! Okay.'

Gleefully Shunya poured the tea into the glass, slurped it down, and licked his lips.

Everyone was silently staring at him. Kumar said to himself, 'I have come to the wrong place, I think. He seems to be a madman, but didn't the monk say that some sages behave in peculiar ways? Let me wait and see.'

An old man sitting in the first row started crying and moaning, 'Terrible back pain, Saami. If I sit for just ten minutes, it begins. Can't walk ten steps. I had to be carried here. Even when I lie down, it doesn't stop. Torture, Saami, it is terrible! I tried to keep quiet but I can't. Saami, please help, Saami, it's worse than death.'

'Stop it!' shrieked Shunya, 'Am I a doctor? Or a vaidya? Don't disturb the silence. What silence? No silence.'

'Saami, please, I beg you...'

Shunya sprang up from his seat and, in one quick move, pulled the old man to standing position, turned him around and hit him so hard on the back that he went tumbling over the man sitting behind him.

'That's what you need,' shouted Shunya, and resumed his seat. Sadasivan and his assistant ran to help the old man, who looked dazed and had stopped screaming.

'This is indeed the wrong place,' Kumar was thinking when Shunya asked the old man who was now standing before him, 'Any pain now?'

'No, Saami,' he said, looking shocked and disoriented.

'Go home. It will not come back again. And don't ever come back to me with such silly complaints.'

There was utter silence. The old man went back to his seat. Nobody spoke. Kumar wondered again.

The silence was broken by Shunya.

'You idiot there, searching for the truth, didn't you find it in America? Still searching?'

Kumar realised that Shunya was addressing him. The sharp eyes seemed to be piercing his heart. How did he know about America? I haven't spoken to anyone, thought Kumar.

'You, say something,' said Shunya.

'Saami,' was all that Kumar could bring himself to say.

'What, saami? Come and sit in the front.'

Kumar trembled with fear and anxiety as he moved towards the front row. All eyes were upon him.

'No, no, come here and sit in front of me,' said Shunya.

Kumar found himself sitting a few feet away from the strange man.

'Closer.'

Now he was at touching distance, and the touch came in a strange way, the healing touch. Without warning, Shunya stretched out his hand and gently stroked his shoulder.

'Poor fellow, no father, no mother, nobody,' he said, 'but you have no-thing, me! You stay with Shunya, my boy, don't go anywhere. No need to wander.'

Suddenly, Kumar's body began to shake. He wept like he had never done before. All the grief that had remained bottled inside him now burst forth. Shunya held his hand, and wiped Kumar's tears with the end of his own loincloth, saying, 'It's nothing, nothing, let everything come out. Empty yourself. Shunya Thambi, Void Thambi.'

From that day onwards, Kumar became Shunya's shadow. Everyone called Kumar Thambi, which meant 'younger brother' in Tamil. Only Sadasivan knew his original name but he, too, called him Thambi. Kumar was dead and Thambi was born. Later on, some people began to call him 'Thambi Saami'.

After Shunya had instructed Sadasivan to let Thambi sleep in the cottage with him at night, and be his companion during the day, the meeting was concluded for the day. Sadasivan announced, 'The satsang is over. Since Saami has not selected anyone to meet him during the week, there will be no interviews this week. In case of an emergency, please contact me. The next satsang is on Tuesday. Salutations, namaskaram!'

The crowd dispersed.

Sadasivan said to Thambi before leaving, 'You are lucky. Nobody has been allowed to sleep in the cottage with Saami. You are young and strong. Look after Saami. See, he is so old. I'll get a pillow and a mat for you. If you need anything, don't hesitate to ask.'

'What are you whispering there?' shouted Shunya. 'Go, Sadasiva. Come here, Thambi.'

Kumar felt as though he had been cleaned and

overhauled. He still wasn't sure what was going to happen, but this was no ordinary man. Something powerful and full of love seemed to dwell inside him. Kumar couldn't define what it was and probably never would, but from then on he became the Void's appendage.

13

Thambi sat and looked at Shunya, wondering how his orthodox father and mother would have reacted to a guru who lived in a toddy shop. Then he remembered his father reading out Vivekananda's writings to him when he was a child. The famous monk had talked about the great sages, known as Paramahamsas, who lived as they liked, ate what they liked and behaved like madmen.

Shunya turned to him and said, 'Ah! Caught your thought just now. Shunya is so clear that nothing escapes it. Orthodox South Indian Brahmins are vegetarians, Bengali Brahmins eat fish, and Swami Vivekananda ate everything. Do you know that? All rubbish, this religion of the kitchen. Don't eat this, don't touch that. What comes out of your mouth is more important than what goes in. Even vegetables have life. You don't want to kill and eat? Nonsense, I say.

'And if you thought a vegetarian diet would make one kinder, well, Hitler was a vegetarian. You are a kind fellow yourself. Be a vegetarian if you want to, but don't point fingers at others who are not.

'Now go and come back after eating something. You may have a bath in the temple pond. It's not far from here. Sadasivan will guide you.'

'Saami, do you need anything?'

'Nothing, nothing.'

At 9 o'clock, Thambi returned with a mat and a pillow that Sadasivan had given him. Shunya was waiting for him outside the cottage.

'Did you eat?'

'Yes Saami, rice, aviyal and rasam.'

Shunya laughed loudly and said, 'Sit down near Zero. Be careful. You also might become a zero.'

They sat quietly looking at the clear night sky. From behind the leaves of the tall coconut palms peeped a thin crescent-shaped moon. Pinpoints of light were scattered all over the sky, some twinkling, some still.

That night, there was no further talk between them except the single sentence uttered by Shunya, 'Come in and sleep beside me in the cottage. Have no fear.'

The cottage contained no furniture. In one corner was a clay water pot with drinking water, and a steel mug. Next to the pot was a folded white towel on which rested a bamboo-reed flute. Shunya shut the door, left the window open and switched off the single electric light.

Thambi spread his mat on the red oxide floor, a little distance away from where Shunya sat on a brown straw mat, and lay down to sleep. A soft breeze came in through the window. A mild fragrance of incense hung in the air.

After a while, a soothing, sweet melody filled the room. It entered his heart, and bathed his entire being in peace. It came from Shunya's direction. In the darkness, he could vaguely discern Shunya sitting up and playing what looked like the flute he had seen in the corner. But he felt no desire to sit up. Listening to the raga, Thambi soon fell asleep and slept soundly.

14

Life went on quietly, or so Thambi thought, but with Shunya one never knew. He seemed crazy, but when it came to dealing with Thambi, Shunya expected him to follow a routine. A schedule was laid out for him. Thambi was to wake up early morning, well before dawn, go out to relieve himself, brush his teeth and meditate with open eyes, watching the sky till it began to light up. Then he would go for a long walk with Shunya in the coconut grove behind the toddy shop. After that, they had a bath in the temple pond, visited the temple sometimes, and returned to the cottage.

After Shunya entered the cottage and shut the door, Thambi was free to go wherever and do whatever he wanted. The only instruction was to not talk too much with anybody.

At night, Thambi, after taking his supper, was instructed to return to the cottage to sleep. 'Every night,' Shunya told him, 'you'll find a black dog called Ponnu sleeping near the jackfruit tree. Sadasivan feeds him daily. Ponnu is my friend. Treat him kindly.'

Ponnu was friendly with Thambi and would lick his hands and feet fondly whenever Thambi sat near him, but until the day Ponnu disappeared, and Sadasivan told him about it, Thambi didn't know that Ponnu was a talking dog.

Soon, Thambi discovered that Shunya never slept.

Since Sadasivan insisted, Thambi ate a little breakfast at around nine in the morning except on Mondays, when the toddy shop remained closed. On Mondays, he fasted in the morning and had only one meal in the evening, which was brought by Sadasivan and Bhavani along with Shunya's food. Thambi stuck to his vegetarian diet and Shunya neither discussed it, nor interfered.

Thambi spent his day reading at the local library, beginning with the writings and speeches of Vivekananda, or went for long walks in the coconut grove and the lush green paddy fields. There was an old, dilapidated and abandoned house with crumbling walls which became his favourite refuge.

When Shunya came out and ate his meal in the evening, Thambi would be at his side, standing or sitting quietly at a respectable distance ready to obey his orders. He did the same when visitors came to see Shunya.

Sadasivan grew to love him like a brother and became his closest friend. 'You are the lucky one,' Sadasivan would never tire of saying.

The second week after Thambi had begun to sleep in the cottage with Shunya, he had a strange and somewhat frightening experience.

He was awakened by an unfamiliar growling sound that seemed to come from above the roof. He saw Shunya sitting on his mat and looking up. The growling grew louder and Thambi's hair stood on end as he saw a round, cannonball-sized blob of brilliant white light coming through the roof. It descended to the ground in front of where Shunya was seated. Then the blob elongated itself into a fearsome shape that could only be described as a yellowish brown, furry, ape-like creature about nine feet high, with a black wolf-like face and long, protruding canines.

Facing Shunya, the creature kept growling at intervals in different pitches and frequencies, and nodding vigorously.

Shunya was doing the same thing, growling and nodding back, and it took some time for Thambi to realise that they were communicating with each other.

Then, Shunya pointed in Thambi's direction, who almost died of fear when the creature turned to look at him for an instant and opened its mouth wide, showing sharp, skewer-like teeth. He wanted to run for the door but fear paralysed him. He could only stare.

Thankfully, in a few minutes, the apparition transformed itself back into a blob of light, and rising high, went through the roof and disappeared. The roof was intact. There was no hole.

As soon as he could recover his wits, Thambi called out, 'Saami.'

'Yes? Come here.'

'Saami, what was that?'

'Nothing, you were hallucinating.'

'No Saami, that was no...'

'Shut up and go to sleep. There are many things in the universe about which they know nothing at the Massachusetts Institute of Technology. MIT, mighty, omniscient scientists, fools. Shut up now and go to sleep. You are safe with me and don't you dare discuss this with anyone.'

Thambi tried to sleep but could manage to do so only for an hour just before dawn.

For one week after that, nothing significant happened. Thambi came to enjoy the daily routine and looked forward to the early morning walks. Sometimes, Shunya was silent throughout. Sometimes, he encouraged Thambi to ask questions.

And then, on one such morning walk, a drama was

enacted which for a short while shook Thambi's faith in Shunya's sanity and credibility to its very foundation.

Shunya was in one of his sullen moods and they had been walking for about fifteen minutes when they saw Ammini, the pregnant daughter-in-law of the Brahmin priest of the temple of the tiger-riding goddess Durga. She had just finished her morning bath in the temple pond, and was wearing a mundu and a red blouse.

'Ah!' shouted Shunya, stopping her in her tracks. 'So you are with child. When is your due date?'

'Two or three days, the doctor says,' she said reluctantly.

'No, no, today, in half an hour,' said Shunya. 'You have such beautiful and full breasts. What a pity.'

Before she or Thambi could recover from the shock of what he had said, Shunya, like a madman, put one arm around her shoulders and using the other hand ripped open her blouse with a tug, uncovered her breasts, and with a lightning-like movement, put his lips to her nipples and sucked hard. 'Milk poison, milk salty,' he said and spat something out.

'What are you doing, Saami?' shouted Thambi, trying to pull him away, but Shunya repeated the act three times. The girl screamed loudly.

Three men ran to her rescue. One was her own father, the other was a passer-by, and the third was the local dhobi.

Together, they dragged Shunya away and threw him to the ground. The father of the frightened girl, now joined by her husband, led her away. By then, more people had gathered.

'Beat up the madman,' someone said.

'I told brother Sadasiva that this fellow is crazy,' said someone else. "Holy man, Saami," he said. "Holy man, my foot."'

'Call the police,' said a third.

Shunya leapt from the ground and, with the agility of a monkey, climbed up a fully grown coconut tree. Sitting up there, he kept shouting, 'Milk, milk, no more, drink as much as you like.'

Thambi, who had been rooted to the spot, suddenly broke into a run. He had to find Sadasivan. The crowd was surely going to beat up Shunya, and he had to save him. Madmen were not responsible for their acts, but was he really mad?

In ten minutes, he was knocking on Sadasivan's door, and explaining what had happened to him and Bhavani.

By the time they arrived at the scene, many people had gathered under the tree. Sub-inspector Chandu Nair and three constables were also present. Shunya, meanwhile, was still seated up in the tree.

As soon as he saw Sadasivan, the inspector said, 'Aah! So the great devotee has come. Didn't I warn you before?' 'And you,' he said to Thambi, 'a disciple in the making, yeah? They say you saw him in the act. Once I get this fellow down, you come with me and give a statement or I'll skin you alive. Can somebody find a toddy-tapper to climb up and bring the rascal down?'

'It cannot be,' said Sadasivan, 'there has to be a different explanation. Saar, please spare Saami.'

'What explanation? What would you have said if he had raped her? I tell you, he is a sex maniac.'

'You watch out too. Don't go too close to him,' said the inspector to Bhavani.

'Inspector saar, I know how to look after my wife,' Sadasivan retorted angrily.

By 11 a.m., they had found a toddy-tapper. Chankaran looked up and wondered how to get Shunya down.

'What if he attacks me up there?' he asked.

'No, he won't.'

'How do you know?'

Just then, the woman's father, brother and husband, accompanied by Kunjan Namboodiri, pushed through the crowd.

'Inspector saar,' said Kunjan Namboodiri, 'we think Saami must be allowed to go unharmed.'

There was silence for a full minute before the inspector spoke. 'What kind of a request is that? The girl was almost...'

'No sir,' said the father, 'we think the situation is different from what it seems.'

'Are you drunk?' asked the inspector, 'or has someone bribed you?'

'I told you...,' started Sadasivan.

'You shut up,' said the inspector.

'Let me explain, sir,' said Kunjan Namboodiri. 'I have known this family well. This girl has had an adverse planetary influence for many years. According to her horoscope, all her children would die the moment she suckled them. Three times in the past, the child she had given birth to died the moment it drank its mother's milk.

'Half an hour after today's shocking episode, she gave birth to a healthy baby girl, who has been breastfed two times now, and is still alive and kicking. Normally, children don't drink milk until a day or so after birth, but this one started straight away. We believe it is Saami's power at work.

'Ammini said that Saami kept repeating, "Milk poison, milk poison," and kept sucking and spitting it out. She thought he was raving mad. Now that her fourth child has survived, we are convinced that Saami was sucking out the poisonous milk to save the child. We have come to plead that he be left unharmed.'

The inspector looked more stunned than anyone else. Recovering his voice and shutting his mouth which had fallen open, he said, 'If a First Information Report had been registered, I wouldn't have let this fellow go. I can't believe this.' Looking up at Shunya, he said, 'You have escaped again but don't think you are too smart. I am going to watch you carefully.'

'Come on, you fellows,' he said to the constables, 'let's go. All you people, now disperse. Let him find his own way to get down from the tree. Wonder how he went up in the first place.'

With that, everyone except the priest, his son, son-in-law, Kunjan Namboodiri, Sadasivan, Bhavani, Thambi and the toddy-tapper, Chankaran, walked away.

'Nice coconuts,' said Shunya from above, 'I won't pluck them!' Then swiftly he climbed down the coconut tree in the style of a toddy-tapper.

'How did you like that? Am I good?' he asked Chankaran after he'd reached the ground.

'As good as any toddy-tapper, Saami,' said Chankaran.

'Don't any of you dare touch my feet,' Shunya warned.

All of them saluted him with folded hands. 'I would like to learn many things from you, Saami,' said Kunjan Namboodiri, 'I am sorry for not realising your greatness. Can I come and see you?'

'Come, come, but I am not sure I have anything to give you. Shunya, nothing, zero. What can Zero give you? But come if you feel like it.'

'Saami, let's go,' said Sadasivan.

'Are you my guardian? Aah! Bhavani, you poor girl,

don't cry. You'll also fulfil your heart's desire. Hey Thambi, self-appointed disciple. Let's go, come.'

Thambi sighed in relief and walked with him to the cottage. Shunya entered the cottage and shut the door. Thambi went to have his bath, ate some breakfast and then went to the library.

'Good that you came and called me,' said Sadasivan, as he turned to leave, 'Saami is God, I tell you.'

God knows, said Thambi to himself, still somewhat dazed.

15

The following week, Shunya, for the first time, had a long and serious dialogue with Thambi during their morning walk, after which Thambi drank a glass of toddy for the first and last time in his life.

That morning, Shunya said to Thambi, 'Ask, ask, clear your mind, don't be lazy.' Thus goaded into questioning, Thambi asked, 'Saami, should I drink toddy? Sada annan very often offers me toddy. I haven't had any so far.'

'No, not if you don't want to.'

'But Sada annan says you wouldn't mind. I am asking you because you are my guru.'

'Oho! You think I am your guru? Even if I were, and you want to do what I do, it makes no sense for you to drink toddy because I don't. Even if I did, imitating me is not the way, absolutely not. Follow the teacher's guidance, but do not imitate him for he acts in different ways, for reasons you cannot comprehend.

'Would you suck a young woman's breast because I did so?'

'No, Saami.'

'Now listen to this story. Once a sage, a madcap zero like me, was walking down the street with his followers. As he passed the local tavern, the owner of the tavern stood by the door saluting him.

"Aren't you going to invite me in?" asked the sage.

"I just prayed that you would grace my tavern," said the man, "but I dare not ask you openly since you are a holy man, and holy men do not enter pubs and taverns."

"Wrong!" said the sage, "a holy man goes everywhere. And anyway, we are drunks too. We drink something so strong that the ordinary man will go berserk with one sip. We are eternally intoxicated. Be that as it may, may I come in?"

'The owner of the tavern, beside himself with joy and gratitude, kissed his hand and led him in. The followers followed.

'Seating him at a comfortable table, he asked most respectfully, "Master, what can I offer you?"

"Whatever you have," said the sage.

"I only have wine," said the man.

"Then so be it," said the sage.

'He offered the sage the best of wines in the best of goblets. Seeing the sage apparently enjoying himself, the followers imitated him and indulged themselves.

'The sage thanked his host and walked out as steadily as he had walked in, while his followers tottered out, inebriated. Not a word was spoken. After a while they reached a foundry where lead was being melted. The owner of the foundry came out and respectfully requested the sage to step in and bless his factory. The sage readily accepted. The followers followed him.

"'Now,' since I am thirsty and you have nothing else to offer, give me some molten lead to quench my thirst," said the sage. He then dipped a crucible into the hot, molten lead, and drank it quietly.

'Turning to his followers he said, "Have your fill."

'Could the stupid followers do it? Could they imitate the master? Think deeply about this, Thambi.'

That evening, while eating his meal, Shunya summoned Sadasivan.

'Bring me some fish,' he said. Sadasivan, happy that his Saami was asking for fish, quickly brought some to him.

'Eat this,' Shunya said, pushing a piece of fish into Thambi's mouth. Thambi ate without a moment's hesitation.

'Good?'

'Smells bad.'

'Nothing smells worse than decaying cadaver. Now you don't need to eat fish, okay? Eat only if you want to.'

'Sadasiva, bring me some toddy,' Shunya instructed. Sadasivan brought a bottle and poured toddy into a glass, wondering what Saami was up to.

'Here, drink soma juice,' Shunya said, taking a sip and passing the glass to Thambi.

Thambi was drinking toddy for the first time. He didn't like it at all, neither the smell nor the taste, but he emptied the glass and gave it back to Shunya. For a short while, he thought he was going to throw up, but the feeling passed.

'How do you feel?'

'Strange.'

'You don't need to drink toddy after this but toddy isn't poison. Let those who drink, drink. Don't bother them. For many hardworking, simple people, alcohol is the only way to an altered state of consciousness. But if you see me drink toddy ever, understand that it is for reasons you cannot comprehend and don't imitate me. This is the mystery of Shunya. Everything pours into nothingness, Shunya, and yet nothing remains, nothing. You'll find out eventually. Go, eat something and come back to sleep.'

Sadasivan smelled the toddy in Thambi's breath and said, 'So Thambi Saami has also started to drink nectar. Come, have your dinner. Shall I bring you some more toddy?'

'No,' said Thambi, 'this was just prasad, consecrated food given by the master. No more.'

After his meal, he went back to the cottage and lay down not too far from Shunya.

Almost instantaneously, he fell asleep.

'Poor boy, poor boy,' whispered Shunya, sitting beside him and softly stroking his hair.

16

One Wednesday afternoon, Kunjan Namboodiri was granted an interview. As he entered the courtyard, Thambi stood up to leave.

'You stay here,' said Shunya.

'But Saami, I want a private...,' began Namboodiri.

'Either he stays or you leave!'

'Okay, Saami, if you say so.'

Shunya was drinking his black tea, sitting under the jackfruit tree. 'Sit here in front of me,' he directed Namboodiri, 'and you, Thambi, sit on his right. Perfect, and listen carefully.'

'Saami,' began Namboodiri, 'I have never met anybody like you. I have met many monks and yogis, magicians, highly learned people, but you are different.

'All the pride that I had in my knowledge of the Vedas and the Shastras has been snuffed out after seeing you. You seem so much like a madman but I sometimes wonder if you are the one who is mad, or we, who are blinded by our desires for name and fame and run hither and thither.

'I have studied the Vedas and the commentaries of Shankara, Ramanuja, Madhawa and others. I have studied the tantras, I have practised the mysterious and secret kundalini yoga, I have studied and understood the mysteries of the planetary positions, I have done everything in this field. You name it and I would have done it, and yet peace evades me. The ultimate truth that the Upanishads talk about is nowhere in sight. I am not free. I pretend to others that I am talking from experience, but I am merely quoting from books.

'What else should I do to grasp the ultimate truth, the Brahman, wherein lies eternal peace and freedom? Can you help me, Saami?'

'Fool,' said Shunya, 'I must go.'

'But Saami, you told me to come. Don't go away, please.'

'The "I" must go. I, I, I, aren't you tired of saying I? That "I" is the problem. Throw it off. That "I" is to be pushed out like shit. All your insides are constipated with ego. Take an enema. Break your image. Get the shit out.

'First, stop chattering, "I did this, I did that, did, did, did." Can you sit quiet for a moment doing nothing? Not this, not this, what then? Nothing, no-thing. Sit quiet, sit silent, be still. Stop doing. Shunya, nothing, clean slate, unalloyed joy!'

Kunjan Namboodiri became silent. Tears flowed down the corners of his eyes which were now closed. The quiet that silently suffused the air was tangible. Thambi felt it too. Shunya broke it by shouting loudly, 'Enough, enough. You'll get it, provided you do what Zero says.'

'Yes, Saami.'

'Anything? You'll do anything to break the ego?'

'Yes, Saami.'

'Okay then, drink toddy. Thambi, bring some toddy for Namboo. Tell Sadasivan, "Nalla kallu."'

When the toddy was brought, Shunya poured it into a glass and held it out to Namboodiri, saying, 'Drink, Tirumeni, this is abhisheka, baptism by the holy spirit. Wash out all your sins.'

Namboodiri drank for the first time in his life. Shunya poured out more. He drank that too without reserve. One bottle was finished.

'Now go home. Some people will say, Tirumeni is drunk, he is finished. What will you say?'

Kunjan Namboodiri stood up and swayed a little. 'I'll say, "Yes, I am drunk. Shunyam got me drunk. I am in ecstasy, I am free." I don't care what others think. I am nothing. I am bliss. *Anandoham, anandoham.*'

'*Bale, besh,* great, wonderful. You are no more a Namboodiri now. You are a human being, a bird that has broken free of the golden cage at last. Go home now, and no more drinking. This is the first and last time. You are permanently drunk. No need for toddy.'

Kunjan Namboodiri danced his way home and lost all his clients.

'Thambi,' said Shunya, after Namboodiri had left, 'you buy yourself a notebook and write down all you saw and heard since you came here, in English.'

'Saami, what if I don't remember correctly and make mistakes?'

'Rascal, do what is asked of you. Do it carefully. No mistakes. Now go and eat your food. It is fuel for the machine. Then come back to sleep.'

That was how Thambi started keeping notes. He was astonished at the clarity with which he remembered every detail as he sat down to write. He seemed to forget nothing.

17

On one occasion, Thambi was woken up in the middle of the night by the sound of someone speaking English. He found Shunya sitting up on his mat. What surprised Thambi was not that Shunya was awake, because he had begun to believe that Shunya never slept, but that he seemed to be having an argument with an invisible person in English. The other person spoke in a gruff, masculine voice, with an American accent, 'You have to guide that asshole professor a bit. It's time now.'

Shunya replied in English with the same drawl and style as the other voice, 'Give him some more time. Or why don't you guide him, Timmy?'

'No, no, you must. He is quite interesting and maybe useful.'

'Okay, send the fellow. I'll make him eat dirt.'

'Oh! Don't be so hard on him, Shunya.'

'Bet your ass, I will.'

With that, the conversation stopped. Shunya said to Thambi in Malayalam, 'He's gone. He's an old friend. We'll soon receive an American visitor, a professor. Now go back to sleep, boy.'

Four days later, Bob Hawkins arrived. He was a professor of philosophy and religion, well-versed in Sanskrit, Arabic and Hebrew, with three published books on Vedanta, Kabala and Sufism to his credit. He was well-travelled and familiar with the Indian subcontinent. At fifty, he boasted of having visited India fifteen times.

Originally a distinguished student of science, he

had majored in quantum mechanics from a well-known American university. He earned his doctorate in the study of tachyon. But at twenty-five, he changed track completely and went back to the university to study religion, philosophy and psychology. In academic circles, he was considered an authority on eastern mysticism.

Timothy Davies, the librarian at the university he taught in, with whom Dr Hawkins had spent many an enjoyable evening discussing Indian philosophy, had told him before he had left for India that year, 'Bob, don't forget to meet the eccentric Shunya Saami. He is not so well-known yet, but you'll find him. He lives behind some kind of a pub in Tirumala, in the suburbs of Thiruvananthapuram, the capital of Kerala. You'll love Thiruvananthapuram. Beautiful beaches, lush vegetation and lovely seafood.'

Bob often marvelled at how Timmy knew India so well, considering that he had never travelled to that country. He'd jotted down the information.

After spending fifteen days in solitude in the upper reaches of the Himalayas, as was his annual practice for the last so many years, Bob was travelling through the southern part of the country. He was in Madras when he remembered Timmy mentioning the eccentric chap in Tirumala. He checked his diary and there it was: Shunya Saami, Tirumala, a suburb of Thiruvananthapuram.

He had never been to Kerala. This time, he decided he would go and meet Shunya.

The next evening, he took a flight to Thiruvananthapuram. From the quaint little airport, he drove down in a rickety old cab to the only good hotel in town, The Mascot Hotel. It was a relic from the colonial era. The rooms were large and as comfortable as they could be, with ancient, groaning fans and squeaking sofas, and water closets that required a great deal of effort to flush. He ate a delicious vegetarian dinner brought to the room by a bearer, turbaned and dressed like a decadent prince. Being tired, he went to bed early.

In the morning, he called the hotel's reception for a cab and explained to the driver where he wanted to go. The cabbie knew how to get to Tirumala. He had even heard vague rumours about Shunya Saami. 'We'll find out, sir,' he said, 'if he lives near a bar, and I think probably a toddy shop, it won't be difficult. Tirumala may have only one.'

So they went to Tirumala, which was not too far away. The cab driver located the toddy shop. Sadasivan, who had just opened the shop, was astonished to see a foreigner looking for Saami.

In broken English, he told Bob to wait. 'Sit on bench, saar,' he said, 'Thambi, English know. Wait.' Though the driver had been paid, he hovered around, curious to see who the sahib had come to see all the way from America and why.

Thambi came in after his walk with Shunya and saw Prof. Hawkins.

'Sahib has come to see Saami,' said Sadasivan.

'Please, sir, be seated, I'll inform Saami,' said Thambi, speaking in English, and hurried towards the cottage.

Bob was not surprised to see this dhoti-clad, bearded young man speak English. He had seen stranger things in India.

Fortunately, Shunya hadn't gone in and locked the door behind him. He was standing under the jackfruit tree looking up at the ripe fruits.

'Saami, that American professor you spoke of has come. Shall I ask him to come back in the evening?'

'Talk to him. Show him your notes. At noon, ask Sadasivan to give him food. Bring him here at 7 o'clock. Today is Tuesday, the day of the general satsang. Other fellows will also come.'

Thambi returned and explained the situation to Bob. 'Fine,' said Bob, 'let's go and have a cup of tea somewhere if it's okay with you.'

'Sure,' said Thambi.

There was a small tea shop close by. Bob and Thambi sat on the bench, sipping tea and talking. Other tea-drinkers and passers-by looked curiously at them. They discussed the white man's appearance among themselves and with the tea-maker, who was busy mixing the tea and the milk, pouring it from one glass to the other, back and forth.

'I think he has come to see Shunya,' said one.

'Yeah, he seems to be getting famous,' said another.

'That fellow with the beard, they say he is his disciple.'

'Young fellow, he should be doing honest labour, able-bodied lazy bum.'

'God knows what the racket is.'

'Why is it taking so long today?' someone shouted. 'One tea here, this is the fourth time I am asking.'

'Coming, coming,' muttered the tea-maker.

∽

After tea, Thambi and Bob walked to the coconut grove. 'I am going to the local library,' said Thambi. 'What would you like to do?'

'I'll just sit there on that stone bench near the pond,' said Bob. 'Please call me as soon as you return.'

'Here, sir, read this. Notes that I have made about my

experiences here. Saami hasn't forbidden me from sharing them with anybody. Anyway, it's in English.'

'Thank you, Thambi, and don't call me sir, okay? Just say Bob, and how come you speak such good English? Tell me about yourself sometime, if you feel like it.'

'Okay, sometime, if you want to know. See you, Bob.'

Thambi went off to the library. Bob sat reading Thambi's notes. 'Fascinating,' he said to himself, 'interesting.'

Thambi returned at one o'clock. He and Bob went to the toddy shop to have lunch. Some of the tables were occupied. Sadasivan found a quiet corner for them. One of the shop's patrons, his speech slurring, said loudly, 'Sada anna, what ish that stange bird that came in with Ambi?'

Sadasivan gave him a hard, long stare.

'Toddy, sir?' asked Sadasivan, moving towards Bob.

'Sure, a little bit. Never had the stuff before,' said Bob.

'Fish curry, mutton? Very good.'

'No, I am a vegetarian. Chappati, dal?'

'Dosa, good dosa, sambar, coconut chutney?'

'Okay.'

The food arrived at their table. Bob drank just a glass of toddy. He didn't like it very much. 'I don't know if I should tell you this,' said Thambi, 'Saami knew you were coming.'

'I was just going to ask you,' said Bob, 'about that entry in your notebook about the night when...what do you call him? Aaaah...Saami. You write Saami spoke to an invisible being in American English; are you sure he said Timmy? Because if it was Timmy, I'll have to do a bit of deep thinking.'

'I thought he said Timmy. Why?'

'Well, I can't tell you now. Maybe later. Anyway, what an extraordinary man, if what you have written is true.'

'You mean you don't believe it is true?'

'No, no. It's just that I have read a lot of biographical material about saints and sages in India. You guys have a great deal of imagination which sometimes leads to exaggeration and before you know it, it's no more a biography, it's a hagiography.

'This is a little different. I think you have tried to say just what you saw and heard yourself. But I was just double-checking.'

In the afternoon, since Bob insisted on going back to the hotel, Thambi helped him hire a cab. Bob promised to be back before seven in the evening.

18

At 7 p.m., about thirty people were seated in the courtyard. Sadasivan and Thambi had reserved a place in the front row for Bob. The door of the cottage opened and Bob set his eyes on Shunya for the first time.

Shunya's eyes darted in all directions except his. Bob felt he was being deliberately ignored. Finally, they rested on him.

'Great professor, learned man,' he said in English. Those who knew English smiled to show that they understood but most of the gathering looked surprised. None of them had expected Saami to know English. They whispered among themselves, 'What is he saying?' Shunya then noticed Bob's camera.

'Oh! Camera,' he shouted, as excited as a little child, 'good, good, kollaam.'

Ammini, the daughter-in-law of the Brahmin priest, the one he had been charged with molesting, was there with her child. Shunya saw her and said, 'Oh ho! The little girl has come. Have you named her?'

'No, Saami,' said her husband, 'my wife Ammini says you have to name her.'

'Yes, Saami,' she nodded.

'Name, name, unhh! Ayesha, that's a good name, beautiful.'

After a short silence, the father of the child spoke, 'Saami, that is a Muslim name. We...'

'Muslim name, Hindu name, what's in a name? You wanted a name from me? That is the name I am giving. It means "alive" in Arabic.'

'Okay, Saami, we shall call her Ayesha,' said the mother, hesitantly looking at her husband.

Shunya smiled, 'That's the spirit, my child. Let us break these imaginary walls.'

The baby shook its hand and said 'Aaaaaa.'

'She understands,' said Shunya, and everybody laughed.

The father said, 'She is as much your daughter as ours, Saami. We shall keep the name.'

Shunya suddenly turned to Bob, 'So, professor, what is your name?'

'Bob, sir.'

'Bobbing up and down the river. Who saved you, Bob? Shunya, nothing.'

Shunya's words fell like a thunderbolt on Bob's head and stirred up long-forgotten memories. As a child of four, he had been washed down a river at a picnic spot in California, and had been given up for dead. The next morning, they found him on the banks of the river, ten miles away, safe and sound. Nobody knew how.

'Hey, Bob,' he heard Shunya saying, as he snapped out of his reverie.

'Sorry, sir, I got lost thinking of something that happened many years ago.'

'Yeah, yeah, the river. Now tell me, why the camera? You are going to take a snap?'

'Only if you don't mind, sir.'

'Don't mind?' He flew into a rage. 'You think I am a cabaret dancer? Should I pull off my mundu and dance before you naked? Bring that camera here.'

Nobody dared say a word.

Bob stood up. Walking towards Shunya, he quietly handed over the expensive camera to him. Shunya stood up with the camera in his hands, raised it to his eyes, looked through the viewfinder and gave it back to Bob.

'Move ten feet away and take a picture,' he said, leaning against the jackfruit tree. 'Is the light okay?'

'Yes, sir,' said Bob, quickly taking a photograph and thanking Shunya.

Then Shunya said, 'Now go back to your seat, Professor Bob.'

A dark young man, in jeans and a yellow t-shirt, stood up and said, 'Saami, I am a journalist from a reputed Malayalam magazine. Can I also take a photograph?'

A camera was slung over his shoulder.

'No, take a copy from Bob and come and see me tomorrow morning at ten. Bob, you come with him. Special interview. Now get out of here or I'll break your camera.

'That's all, satsang over, dursang over, go home, everybody. Shunya to be left alone. Bob, come in the morning.'

Everyone dispersed. Bob said goodbye to Thambi, hired a cab and went back to the hotel. He had a light dinner, read for a while, and then tried to sleep.

The image of himself as a panic-stricken child being washed away by a turbulent river kept coming back to him every time he closed his eyes. He couldn't sleep.

At midnight, he called up room service. A sleepy voice answered. 'Can I get some toddy?' Bob asked.

'What, sir? Toddy, sir? No toddy, sir, this is Five Star, sir. We have Scotch, sir, Johnnie Walker.'

'That's fine, I don't want a drink. Goodnight.'

Lying on the bed, he meditated on the image of Shunya leaning against the jackfruit tree. Sleep crept in slowly. He dreamt that he was a small child in a cradle, and Shunya, wearing a bright red apron, was rocking the cradle and putting him to sleep singing the nursery rhyme, 'Hickory dickory dock, the mouse ran up the clock.'

19

The next morning, Bob and the journalist, Sukumaran, arrived to meet Shunya. Sadasivan and Thambi led them to the jackfruit tree. Shunya was sitting under the tree, waiting for them.

'Thambi, you stay here, and you too, Sadasiva,' said Shunya, 'and now Bob the bobber and Suku-suku, let's begin. Bob speaks first.'

'Thank you, sir,' said Bob, 'I have heard so much, read so much, practised meditation, and met many yogis and gurus. I read Thambi's notes yesterday and I think I have some kind of a past link with you. Never felt like this before. I am going to ask you a plain question. Did you save me from the river when I was drowning as a child? Or am I imagining it?'

'Shunyam knows nothing. Can nothing save something?'

'All right, if you don't want to answer that question, that's fine, but the most important question is, when will I attain moksha, liberation, realisation? Please answer my question.'

'Sadasiva, bring me some black tea,' ordered Shunya.

Sadasivan ran to fetch some tea. Sukumaran, the journalist, said, 'Saami, I wanted to...'

'Shut up, not now,' said Shunya.

Sadasivan returned with a kettle and a glass, and placed them in front of Shunya, who began pouring the tea. The glass was full to the brim, but Shunya continued to pour. The tea overflowed and ran down the stone slab, but Shunya poured. No one dared say a word. Shunya kept pouring. Suddenly Bob exclaimed, 'Sir, the glass is full!'

'Hah! Your glass is full, professor,' said Shunya, 'how can I give you moksha? Your brain is full. It is full of shit. No space to pour in anything new. Anything I pour will overflow and get wasted, understand?'

He put away the kettle, emptied the glass at one go, and said, 'Ah! Pretty strong, Sadasiva, good stuff but put in a little more jaggery next time.'

Bob said, 'Sir, I want to confess something.'

'In front of all these people?'

'I don't mind.'

'Okay, talk. Go on.'

'Sir, I have been experimenting with drugs.'

'What drugs? Ganja, cannabis indica? Hemp, same plant from which hashish is made. Psychoactive drug, they call it. The Hashishin were a bunch of hashish addicts, suicide squads, programmed to kill for their religion. The word assassin comes from 'hashishin'. Holy terrorists! Deprogramme yourself, empty the shit, purge.'

Bob said, 'I have also tried stronger drugs, sir, the sacred Mexican mushroom...'

'Fly agaric, manna from heaven, god's footstool,' said Shunya.

'Yes, sir, and LSD. My friend George Leary thought it altered the state of consciousness forever. It did give me some insights, but nothing changed permanently.'

'Do you still use LSD?'

Bob remained silent for a moment, and then said almost in a whisper, 'Yes, sir, sometimes.'

'Are you carrying some with you now?'

'As a matter of fact, yes.'

'Show me.'

Bob put his fingers into the small leather pouch

attached to his belt and brought out a bottle with tiny white tablets inside it.

'How do you use it?' asked Shunya.

'You dissolve one tablet in a glass of water,' said Bob, 'then soak a piece of blotting paper in the water, and put the paper on your tongue to let the drug dissolve. That's enough for one trip for a normal person. An overdose might lead to mental derangement and even death.'

'Ah! So strong, and how many are there in the bottle?'

'About twenty, sir. They are very expensive.'

'Let me see. Give me the bottle.'

Bob gave him the bottle.

'Unhum! Nice tablets, beautiful, beauty-fool,' said Shunya and opening the lid emptied the contents into his cupped left hand. Then throwing the empty bottle away, he proceeded to count the tablets.

'Twenty-five,' he counted, blew three times softly on them and turned to Bob. 'Now, Bob Sahib is going to have them all at once.'

'Good God!' exclaimed Bob.

'What now?' asked Thambi.

'I don't know,' said Bob, looking very frightened and disturbed, 'that's enough to kill a person in a few minutes.'

'Come, Bob,' said Shunya, 'come here, open your mouth.'

Bob obeyed like a child.

'Sadasiva, bring me some water,' said Shunya. Sadasivan handed Shunya a glass.

Shunya dropped all the tiny little tablets into Bob's mouth, handed the glass of water to him and said, 'Swallow the tablets.'

Bob did as he was told.

'Now sit quietly in the corner, close your eyes, and chant Ommmm.'

Bob sat down crossed-legged and chanted Om but knowing the lethal effects of an LSD overdose, he was trembling with fear. All eyes were on him. Fifteen minutes passed and nothing happened. Another fifteen minutes and still nothing.

Bob opened his eyes and said, 'I don't understand; that dose is enough to kill a person. I feel fine as of now, Saami.'

Shunya said loudly, 'Aha! You thought you were going to die! Nothing happened. Nothing ever happens. Now Suku can ask questions to Nothing, to Shunya.'

Bob took some time to recover from the shock. Conventional logic did not seem to apply in this case, but he would watch and wait. His rational mind was still reluctant to accept what had happened.

Sukumaran, the journalist, visibly shaken, said, 'I… where shall I begin?'

'Anywhere, newshound, there is no beginning and no end. Start, before I get up and walk away.'

'Saami, maybe it makes no sense to ask you this question,' said Sukumaran, 'but who are you? Where were you born? Who are your parents? Do you want to tell me?'

'Yeah, Shunyam was born from a womb. No immaculate conception. Born of copulation, just like all of you. Nobody falls directly from heaven.

'His parents were humans, not monkeys or gods. Born in Kerala, ate and drank, was a lover, husband, father, scientist, fucker of images, went across the seas and came back empty. Shunyam, free, zero, vacuum, bliss, oh death, where is thy stinking fart?'

'Saami,' said Sukumaran, 'you seem to be a Hindu to us. You visit the temple sometimes, you seem to know the Shastras, and you certainly are not a Muslim.'

'How do you know?' shouted Shunya, flying into a rage, 'what if I was a circumcised Muslim? Have you seen my thing? Investigative journalism! Want to see?'

Taken by surprise, and somewhat scared, no one uttered a word. The rumour that was doing the rounds was that Sadasivan had once seen a shiny crystal penis with a golden-headed cobra coiled around it.

'Any more questions?' asked Shunya.

'Saami, I want to publish an article about you.'

'Do what you want. What will you write about Shunya? About nothing? Interview over now, everyone can go. No more satsangs today. Bob, do you think the tablets were wasted?'

'I don't know, sir.'

'Sadasiva, give Bob a glass of toddy with his lunch. Sukumara, you too. Eat before you leave and have some toddy if you like. Journalists drink, somebody told me, but Shunya needs no toddy. He was born drunk.'

Sadasivan fed Bob and Sukumaran, and gave them a glass of toddy each. Before leaving, Sukumaran collected more information about Shunya from Thambi and Sadasivan.

Bob spent the afternoon and evening sightseeing in Thiruvananthapuram. He visited the old palace and the ancient temple of Anantha, the presiding deity of Tiru-anantha-puram. From his navel grew a lotus. He could only see the temple from outside since non-Hindus were not allowed entry into the sanctum sanctorum. He went to the zoo, the museum and lastly the Shangumukham ('face of the conch') beach. He took photographs, thoroughly enjoyed the trip and returned to his hotel at eight in the evening.

After a soothing cold shower, he switched on the fan and sitting on the bed, tried to meditate. The image of Shunya popping twenty-five LSD pills into his mouth all at once flashed in his mind again and again. At nine-thirty, he called room service and ordered rice, sambar and vegetables for dinner.

'Sir, we also have some toddy for you, the best,' said the waiter. 'You asked for it yesterday.'

'No, not today.'

'Ice-cream, sir, or coffee?'

'Neither, thank you.'

After dinner, he switched on the reading lamp, got into bed and read the local English daily for a while. It was the usual fare: political rallies, thefts, one or two murders, the chief minister inaugurating a statue of Karl Marx in the Communist Party's district office, and so on.

He put away the newspaper and thought of telling Sukumaran to not mention the LSD in the magazine article, since he didn't want any trouble with the customs officers or the police. He also wanted Sukumaran to remind him to hand over a copy of Shunya's photograph. Then he switched off the light and closed his eyes. Just before he fell asleep he had a vision. In his mind's eye, he saw Shunya swallowing the LSD pills. Then, curiously, Shunya transformed himself into Bob's form, minus his clothes, stark naked, still swallowing the tablets.

In the next instant, liquid, pulsating waves of brilliant silvery light broke forth from nowhere and flooded his consciousness. His consciousness was no more confined to his body, it was everywhere. He was the whole undulating universe. Bob was bobbing up and down in a sea of light, drowned in bliss. His mind was no more, and infinite peace which is not of the mind remained. Freedom, emptiness, nothingness! So free!

The blissful state must have lasted the whole night, for when the day broke and light filtered in through the window, Bob woke up as if from a long dream. The Bob who woke up felt different from the one who had gone to sleep. After years of experimenting with LSD, he knew this had nothing to do with the chemical. It was completely different and there was no addictive craving for the next dose.

The ecstasy remained, though it was not so intense, and a sense of lightness suffused his consciousness. The whole world looked beautiful. His brain sought no explanation. It was still, and at peace with itself.

He didn't feel like going to the dining hall. Ordering idlis for breakfast, he showered and changed into a comfortable t-shirt and sat down beside the window. He could see the green wooded area which was the zoo. From somewhere within, a lion's roar rumbled like distant thunder.

ॐ

After breakfast, he walked to the zoo, and buying a ticket, spent the whole day leisurely wandering around it. At four in the evening, as he walked out, he thought of how the animals had to live and die in captivity. Sadly, human beings were no different. They too lived and died in cages of their own making.

He had some sandwiches and coffee at a small

restaurant called the Indian Coffee House, hailed a cab and went directly to the abode of Shunya Saami.

Sadasivan met Bob near the door. 'Thambi, Professor has come,' he called out. Thambi came out and greeted Bob.

'Namaste, Bob, Saami was asking about you. No general satsang today, but he said he would see you when you came.'

'Thanks, Thambi, shall I go to him now?'

'Yes, I think so.'

The time was 5.30 p.m. They found Shunya standing under the jackfruit tree. As soon as he saw Bob and Thambi approaching, he chanted a Sanskrit verse from the Isavasya Upanishad that Bob was familiar with. He then translated the verse into English, 'The Supreme Being pervades everything here. Everything is nothing, Shunya.'

Bob bowed low with his head touching the ground and prostrated himself before Shunya in the Indian way. He said, 'Thank you, sir, thank you very much for last night's experience.'

'Oh! That,' said Shunya, 'it's nothing much. Epileptic seizures of the left temporal lobe can also give you a similar experience. Good, good, stay on for some time. No thanks needed to Shunya. Let Shunya be Shunya. No need for LSD any more. You are drunk without toddy like Shunya. Go for a walk with Thambi.'

So Thambi and Bob went out for a walk in the coconut grove.

20

A series of major changes began to take place in Tirumala. Sadasivan shifted his toddy business to new premises some distance away. The old shop became a dining hall during the day and by night, a dormitory for the visitors who came from afar. Sadasivan had hired a manager for the new toddy shop. He himself was always at the old shop, which was now called the Ashram, looking after the needs of Shunya and his devotees. Skeptics called it the Toddy Ashram, Kallu Ashram.

Sukumaran had published his article in the newspaper by then, and many more people began to gather around Shunya. These included politicians, businessmen, people in search of miraculous cures, journalists from national dailies, spiritual seekers, and those who came simply out of curiosity.

Bob, too, published an article on Shunya in a leading American newspaper, which resulted in the arrival of foreigners. Hotels in Thiruvananthapuram had to be booked for them. Shunya Saami became a famous name and people came from all corners of the world. Shunya remained as unaffected as ever, and just as crazy.

Among those who arrived was Diana Pearce, a young English woman of twenty-six, who had had an unhappy childhood. Her father, a well-known lawyer, had become a cocaine addict and had died when she was just turning eighteen. The same year, her mother married a rich former client of her late husband and moved out of the family home. Diana lost faith in all human relationships and turned into an introvert. Like many others of her generation, she had developed an interest in Indian religions and mysticism, and had taken up the practice of yoga.

Wanting to lead a life conducive to spiritual progress, she had opted out of brilliant career opportunities that had come her way in London, and had gone to live and work in a boarding school in a remote village near Sussex, teaching English. She had become a vegetarian, and everything had gone on well. Then the thunderbolt fell. She began to notice that her appetite was decreasing daily. If she forced herself to eat, she developed severe pains in her abdomen. She was getting weaker by the day because she couldn't hold even small quantities of food inside and began to throw up even liquids.

The local doctor referred her to a specialist in London. The specialist, after going through the test results, informed her that she had intestinal cancer, and that too at an advanced stage. She would survive two more months, he said. He suggested chemotherapy, but it could be painful, and he couldn't guarantee a recovery.

For days she contemplated suicide, and then decided to take the risk and try chemotherapy. During her second visit to London, as she made arrangements for her treatment, she ran into an old friend, Professor William Bryson, who taught philosophy at a British university, and was her late father's client.

Pained to hear of her condition, he said, 'Diana, I don't know if this will help, but I have a good friend, a reliable chap called Bob, actually Prof. Bob Hawkins, who is now visiting southern India. Bob is quite a sceptic so when he wrote to me the other day that he was in touch with a genuine sage, a man he believes possesses what he called healing powers, I was surprised and intrigued. Now if I could get Bob on the telephone, which by itself is quite a feat in India, and if he says it is worth it, would you be willing to go to India? I think it's worth a try. Don't worry about the money. I'll take care of that. Will call you up in a day or two.'

When Prof. Bryson's call came on the morning of the third day after their meeting, Diana had, for some strange reason she herself couldn't fathom, begun to feel strongly that she should go to India. She had decided to give him a call if he didn't get in touch with her by the evening.

Prof. Bryson said that he had contacted Prof. Bob Hawkins in India and everything had been arranged. She had to quickly get herself a visa. He would help her speed up the process using his contacts in the Indian High Commission.

Within a week, her visa was ready. Prof. Bryson handed her a ticket and a thousand pounds. 'Go, my dear, and may God be with you,' he said.

She was to fly from London to Bombay and then to Thiruvananthapuram. Prof. Hawkins would be at the airport to receive her. Diana thanked Prof. Bryson, trying hard to hold back her tears.

21

One Tuesday evening, Diana was escorted to Shunya's presence by Bob. Her condition had worsened. She couldn't even hold water in her stomach.

The general satsangs had been increased to four days a week on account of the unprecedented rush of visitors, and the hall was crowded. Bob and Diana sat in the third row.

As soon as Shunya entered the hall, he looked directly at Diana. 'Come to the front row, both of you,' he said.

The others made way for them.

'Sit down and now tell me.'

'She...,' began Bob.

'Be quiet,' said Shunya, 'let her speak. Thambi, are you there?'

'Yes, Saami.'

'Okay, go on.'

As Diana looked at his kind eyes, all her fear and uncertainty vanished. Starting from the very beginning, she gave a detailed account of everything that had happened to her.

Shunya kept nodding, 'Umph! Umph!'

'...and so, sir,' she said, 'that's what it is. I am going to die; the doctor has given me one month more. I know I am going to die, and there is great pain. And I really don't know why I am here, except for peace of mind, perhaps?'

'So,' said Shunya in a deep voice, 'you are going to die. Then we are in the same boat. I am going to die. He, he, she, all of us,' he gestured with his right hand, 'we are all going to die and, truly, no one knows when. At least you seem to know. One month, did you say? You are better off than the rest of us because you seem to be sure. We are all going to die, maybe now, maybe later, but die we will, so why worry? Relax, be at peace, my dear, be at peace. Come, sit on my lap, come darling.'

There was absolute silence. No one said a word. Diana felt a deep sense of peace and security enter her soul. Without hesitation, she stood up, walked to Shunya and sat on his lap.

Shunya stroked her blonde hair softly, and held her like a mother holds her child. Diana began to cry silently. Her tears drenched Shunya's chest.

'Pavam, pavam, poor thing, poor thing,' he kept saying, 'nothing, nothing, Shunya.'

It took some time for Diana to stop crying and pull herself together.

'Now,' said Shunya, 'go and rest for a while. Sadasiva, Thambi, Bob, take care of this child. Your name is?'

'Diana, sir.'

'Diana, goddess of the moon. Call me "Appa", father.' Then turning to the others he said, 'Satsang is over.'

22

At first, Diana stayed at the Mascot Hotel where Bob resided, but she went there only to sleep. She spent most of the day in the local library with Thambi or walking about in the coconut grove. When it wasn't raining, she sat beside the temple pond with its greenish algae-covered water. Every morning, she and Thambi visited the Shiva temple. She was present at all the satsangs.

Meanwhile, a remarkable change was taking place. Her pain began to lessen, and she could eat and drink small quantities of food without throwing up. In fifteen days, she was able to eat normally. The pain had disappeared.

On the sixteenth day, Shunya called her for a special interview in the morning. Thambi escorted her to Shunya's official seat under the jackfruit tree. The sun was out. The rains had stopped for a while.

'Thank you, Appa,' she said.

'Aha! You are looking beautiful, anh! Thambi, you like her?'

Both Thambi and Diana looked down embarrassedly. Diana blushed. 'Okay, okay, now leave the hotel and stay in Sadasivan's house for some time. You need special food now. I'll talk to Sadasivan later. Thambi, you tell him now. Diana, don't worry, Bhavani, Sadasivan's wife, is a very good girl.'

So Diana went to live in Sadasivan's house. According to Shunya's special instructions to Bhavani, Diana's diet for the next twenty days should not contain salt. In addition, she was to drink a glass of hot cow's milk every night before sleeping.

Bhavani looked after Diana with great love and affection. Diana saw Shunya's photograph being worshipped in the little shrine room in Sadasivan's house. 'Photo by Bob sahib,' explained Bhavani.

By then, Shunya had become well-known, and the crowds swelled day by day. Sadasivan and Thambi had to devise plans to protect Shunya's privacy. They roped in a few others, including Kunjan Namboodiri, who now called himself a devotee.

All visitors had to register their names with a volunteer, who acted as the receptionist. Arrangements for food and lodging were streamlined, and so were the satsangs. The courtyard was extended to accommodate the crowds. There were four general satsangs in a week and nobody was allowed near the cottage at other times, unless Shunya had specifically asked for someone. When Shunya went for his walks in the coconut grove in the mornings with Thambi, guards were posted to make sure that no one disturbed him.

When he was not meeting people, Shunya preferred to remain in solitude in his cottage. Thambi, his constant companion, was the only one who had access to him at all times.

And as it happens always with fame, jealousy and hatred were not far behind. There were all kinds of people who disliked Shunya, who resented his popularity and would have gladly seen him dead.

Here was a man who seemed to have no respect for the establishment, or for organised religion, or for any kind of 'ism', including communism. He was dangerous because he was an iconoclast. He ridiculed 'immaculate conception', lived in a place that sold alcohol, used obscene language, encouraged inter-religious marriages, tried to break the caste system, challenged the theories of Marx, took LSD, or so they heard, and so on and so forth. He sure was a threat to the establishment and its self-appointed guardians.

So, rumours were planted and spread. One version said he was a CIA agent; why else would the Americans be there? Other versions variously labelled him a sex maniac, a tantrik who performed weird Devil worship in his cottage at midnight, a black magician, the Anti-Christ, and so on.

As long as he'd remained confined to Sadasivan's little toddy shop, it was fine, but now he was going global. Distinguished foreigners were fawning on him. Who knew which sacred idol he would set out to topple next?

Anger and jealousy simmered under the surface, waiting for a chance to take revenge.

Of course, there were the wise ones, the so-called intellectuals, who dismissed the phenomenon as just another godman cheating the gullible or, at best, a mere lunatic with luck on his side.

Shunya, however, remained Shunya, 'the nothing', and cared for nothing, and was as free as the wind.

But the unusual, the odd and the miraculous tend to draw attention. The crowds continued to grow, and so did the number of extraordinary stories, which the tellers claimed were authentic.

23

One of these stories came from a boy of six named Appukkuttan. Shunya normally did not interact with children but Appukkuttan was an exception. Shunya first saw him on one of his morning walks, sitting beside the temple pond, bare bodied except for a pair of faded khaki shorts. A pair of large, shining eyes stared at Shunya through partings in the long, black hair that fell over his face.

Shunya, with Thambi in tow, went up to him and asked, 'What is your name?'

'Appukkuttan,' said the boy without any hesitation, 'everybody calls me Appu.'

'Who is your father?'

'Bhaskaran, but I don't remember. He died long ago.'

'Your mother?'

'She died as soon as I was born. I live with my maternal uncle Narayanan. He is a farm labourer and never sent me to school. I don't like school anyway. The cruel teachers beat you up with canes.'

Shunya smiled, 'So what do you do the whole day?'

'I just walk around, throw pebbles into the pond, and sometimes eat vadas in Madhu anna's little tea shop whenever he is in a good mood. My uncle comes back home in the evening and I help his wife cook tapioca and fish curry, and sometimes rice. I enjoy rice and fish curry, you know. Tell me, why are you asking me all these questions?'

'Because I like you,' said Shunya, 'I will see you tomorrow if you happen to come here. Goodbye.'

They walked away with the boy staring curiously at them. The next day, he was there again and as the meetings continued, he became a great friend of theirs.

One morning, Shunya said to Thambi, 'Thambi, you go ahead. I want to be with Appu for a while. We'll meet in the evening.' Thambi walked away.

As Shunya approached the pond, Appu came running towards him. 'Shunya ammava, Shunya uncle,' he shouted, 'I want to ask you something!'

'Go ahead.'

'You said to me the other day, you can take me wherever I wanted to go.'

'Yes.'

'I thought it over and decided that I want to go to Sabarimala.'

Sabarimala was a hill shrine situated in the dense rain forest 200 miles from Thiruvananthapuram. Every year, hundreds of people went on a pilgrimage to the shrine. Those who took the vow to undertake the pilgrimage had to observe celibacy for forty days from the time they wore the consecrated rosary around their necks. They also had to stop shaving and cutting their hair, dress in black or blue, become a vegetarian, and perform the special worship of Ayyappa, the deity of Sabarimala, every day.

On the forty-first day, they would set out, usually in batches, and cover the two hundred mile journey by bus or car. Vehicles stopped a few kilometres away from the foot of the hill. After that, the pilgrims walked barefoot, bathed in the Pampa River and began the climb to the top.

It was a steep and arduous climb that took about two hours for the average healthy male. In the past, tigers and leopards roamed the thick forests. The pilgrims' full-throated cries of 'Swamiyae Saranam Ayyappa' and the beating of drums helped to keep the wild beasts away. Over the years, as human presence multiplied, the animals shied away and disappeared, but the path that wound up the hill remained rough. Especially just after the rains, the road was slippery and full of leeches that attached themselves to the legs of the pilgrims and fattened themselves by sucking their blood, very much like money-lenders and the hordes of priests who hung around holy places in India.

But the Ayyappa Saamis, as the black-clad pilgrims were called, considered all that a penance to please the teenaged celibate god Ayyappa, whose gold idol squatted in a yogic pose in the sanctum sanctorum. As a mark of respect for his celibate status, only women who had reached menopause were allowed to go up the hill.

The last part of the journey was the climb to the sanctum sanctorum. To reach there, the pilgrims had to walk up the eighteen narrow, silver-plated steps that were made dangerously slippery by clarified butter, spilt when the pilgrims who reached the top performed the ritual of breaking coconuts filled with butter by striking them hard on the sharp edge of the last step.

As the pilgrims sighted the handsome golden deity, glorious after a bath of butter, milk, honey and rosewater, and decorated with beautiful flower garlands, emotion-laden, tearful cries of 'Swamiyae Saranam Ayyappa' would burst forth from their throats. The priest, who had to remain celibate for the whole season, would accept the offerings from the devotees and give them back a little bit of the consecrated food to eat and take back home. With hundreds of devotees coming up the hill, each one got only a fleeting glance of the diety before being shooed down by the barefooted, bearded policemen on special duty.

Coming down from the rock-cut steps at the rear, the pilgrims came to a small clearing, which had temporary shacks that served as restaurants. There were also stalls run by the temple committee which sold sweets, five-fold nectar and panchamrit (comprising banana, ghee, jaggery, honey and milk), consecrated food that had been ritually offered to the deity.

The descent took less time than the ascent. In spite of the bruised soles and tired knee joints, there was this tearing hurry to get back to the plains and abandon the vows as quickly as possible. For some this meant finding the nearest toddy shop, for others, it meant eating meat and fish, and for some, breaking out of the celibate mode.

When Appu said, 'I want to go to Sabarimala,' Shunya chanted loudly, 'Swamiyae Saranam Ayyappa, Harihara Sudhanae Saranam Ponnayyappa.' This meant, 'Lord Ayyappa, I surrender to you son of Hari and Hara, golden-hued Ayyappa, I surrender to you.'

The reason why Ayyappa was called 'son of Hari and Hara' went back to a story from the Puranas. It is said that in ancient times, when the cosmos was still young, the celestial beings called Devas, depicted in latter-day paintings as clean-shaven, fair, handsome, ornamented beings, the good Aryan type, and the dark-bodied brutes, the Asuras, the bad ones, who guffawed endlessly and had thick, turned-up moustaches of the kind associated with warriors, villains, dacoits and anti-heroes in general, were at constant war with each other. During a short period of ceasefire, they decided to churn the primordial ocean of milk together in order to obtain the nectar which conferred immortality on the imbiber.

They used the great mountain Meru as the churning

rod and the divine serpent Vasuki as the rope. The serpent was wound around the churning rod and the Asuras and the Devas holding the two ends began to churn the ocean.

The first product that came out of the churning was the lethal hala hala poison which threatened to destroy the cosmos. The great god Shiva, who lived on Mount Kailash, came to their rescue by drinking it. His consort, Parvati, fearing that in the process of saving the universe, her lord would be affected by the poison, squeezed his neck with both her hands so that the poison would not descend to the rest of his body. Shiva's throat turned blue and so he came to be known as Neelakanth, the blue-throated one.

Finally, when the nectar of immortality emerged, the Asuras got hold of the bowl that contained it and started to run away with it.

Vishnu, the great god, sustainer of the universe, who was watching the proceedings and who was himself a clean-shaven, beautiful but infinitely grander replica of the Devas, decided to act.

Vishnu exercised his magic powers and transformed himself into Mohini, a voluptous enchantress. Infatuated by this red-lipped, big-bosomed beauty, the foolish Asuras let go of the bowl of nectar and ran after her. The Devas, meanwhile, got hold of the nectar and partook of it, thereby becoming immortal.

Mohini, by using her magical powers, escaped from the Asuras who were pursuing her and reached a beautiful isolated garden of sweet-scented flowers deep in the forest. There as she was admiring her own beauty, looking at her image on the surface of a clear pond, she realised that Shiva himself, infatuated by her beauty, had followed her to that lonely spot.

As the story of Ayyappa goes, consumed by a passionate and burning desire, Shiva and Vishnu, in the form of Mohini, indulged in conjugal union. Mohini gave birth to a divine boy instantly. Since Vishnu's popular name was Hari and Shiva's Hara, the child came to be known as Hariharasuta, or the son of Hari and Hara. The child was left in the forest only to be discovered and adopted by the King of Pandalam who ruled the territory.

The adopted son, named Ayyappa, grew up to become a courageous, handsome and well-built young man. The queen, fearing that the king, who loved Ayyapa very much, might make him the heir to the throne in place of her own son, schemed to eliminate him.

She pretended to be very ill with severe abdominal pain and the court physician, who was in league with her, declared that she could be cured by drinking tiger's milk, which only Ayyappa was capable of procuring. The king refused to send Ayyappa into the jungle, but he volunteered and persuaded the king to let him go. Ayyappa went into the forest and came back riding a female tigress, which he proceeded to milk.

His divinity was thus proved and after helping the king in a few battles, it is said that he went up the Sabari Hill. There, sitting in a yogic posture, he turned into a golden idol so that those who dared to walk through the jungle, keep their vows and climb the hill could worship him and fullfil their wishes.

In Kerala, Ayyappa is the most popular of the gods and little children are told his story while they are still in their cradles.

Appu had always been fascinated by Ayyappa, but his maternal uncle had declined to take him on pilgrimage to the hill shrine twice. He hoped Shunya uncle would help him.

'Saranam Ayyappa, Hariharasutanae Saranam Ayyappa,' repeated Appu, 'and when will you take me?'

'Today, my boy,' said Shunya, 'come in the afternoon at four to my cottage, and don't tell a soul. Secret! Okay?'

Appu giggled in excitement. 'I will,' he said and ran away.

In the afternoon, Appu knocked on the door of the cottage. Shunya opened the door and let him in. Except for the two of them, there was no one inside. The window was shut and the room was dimly lit by an oil lamp that stood in a corner. Shunya shut the door. 'Nice smell of incense,' said Appu.

'Yes, yes, come, let us not waste time,' said Shunya and kneeled down on the floor in the centre of the room. 'Now you climb up and sit on my shoulders, and clasp your hands around my head.'

Appu did as he was told.

'Good, now close your eyes and no matter what you feel, don't open them. Open them only when I ask you to. Clear?'

'Yes.'

In a few seconds, Appu got the feeling that they were levitating and then moving swiftly through the air. He wondered how they could have come out of the closed room and how people would react if they saw them flying above their heads, but he dared not open his eyes.

While still airborne, Appu heard faint cries of 'Swamiyae Ayyappa' coming from down below and felt as if they were descending. As they descended, the cries became louder until they sounded quite close. Then Appu felt that they had landed on solid ground, but obediently kept his eyes shut tight, waiting for the command. Sure enough, Shunya said, 'Open your eyes and climb down.'

Appu opened his eyes. They were in a small clearing in the middle of a heavily wooded forest. From where they stood, they could see hundreds of pilgrims, filled with devotion, chanting loudly 'Swamiyae Ayyappa' as they trudged up the hill.

'Come,' said Shunya, 'let's join the pilgrims.' He led the way through a small track that climbed uphill, until they joined the pilgrim route at a point not too far away from the shrine. From where they stood, they could see the shrine on the top of the hill. Appu looked at himself and at Shunya and was astonished to see that they too were clad in black and had rosaries around their necks. Joining the chorus and chanting 'Swamiyae Saranam Ayyappa,' they went up the eighteen holy steps to the sanctorum, and had a good look at the golden Ayyappa. They painted their foreheads with the sandalwood paste given by the priest and came down to the place where there were makeshift eateries and stalls that sold the prasad that came from the shrine.

'You must be hungry, and so am I,' said Shunya. They went into an eatery called Annapoorna, and Shunya bought some idli and chutney and some strong hot tea for both of them. After the meal and the customary belching which was a kind of thanksgiving, Shunya took Appu to the stall and bought him some prasad. 'Keep this,' he said, 'and show it to the sceptical. Of course, the hardened ones won't believe you. Now come, we must go. It'll soon be time for satsang at Tirumala.'

Shunya lead Appu back to the place where they had

landed and bade him to climb on his shoulders once again
and keep his eyes shut. Soon, Appu felt airborne again
and in a short while he could feel them descending and
landing on firm ground.

'Open your eyes,' said Shunya. Appu opened his eyes
and found that they were back in the dimly lit cottage.

'Now get down, you are heavier than I'd thought,'
said Shunya.

Appu scrambled down and exclaimed, 'Oh God! We
are no longer dressed in black.'

'But you still have the rosary around your neck. Here,
take this also.' Shunya took his rosary and put it around
Appu's neck. 'Now scram,' he said.

From that day onwards, Appu never tired of telling the
story of his magical trip to Sabarimala. His descriptions
were so graphic that the listeners either thought that he
had actually visited the place and was inventing just that
bit about his mysterious aerial mode of transport, or that
he was merely a great storyteller who had collected all
the details from other pilgrims. The fact that he wore the
rosary did not signify much because such rosaries could
be bought across the counter especially during pilgrimage
season and the prasad could have come from other pilgrims.

Thambi jotted down Appu's story in detail. A small
number of people believed the story in full but couldn't
get confirmation from Shunya. When asked, he merely
said, 'Shunya, the Void, is everywhere; here, there, Saranam
Ayyappa. Appu is a good boy.'

When his maternal uncle came to know of Appu's
friendship with Shunya, he quietly took him away and left
him with his younger sister who lived in the faraway city
of Palghat. His sister was told that Shunya was a dangerous
madman who was influencing young Appu's mind.

So Appu lived with his aunt and continued to tell his
story. When he grew up and married, he told the story
to his bride and took her to see the place where Shunya
had lived. His children heard the story from him and so
did his grandchildren. When Appu was about to die at
the ripe old age of ninety, the last words he uttered were,
'Shunya uncle has come. I must now go to Sabarimala.'

24

One morning, Shunya took Diana along with Thambi for a walk in the coconut grove. They walked silently for a while.

Suddenly Shunya turned to Diana and asked, 'You like Thambi, no?'

Diana, taken by surprise, blushed but kept quiet.

'You, Thambi? You like her?'

'Yes, Saami. I can't keep secrets from you. Is it wrong to like her or think of her?'

'No, no, nothing wrong, but let's see. What do you think Diana, my child?'

'I like him, but…'

'But what?'

'I have cancer, I am a foreigner. Thambi is a fine man and he deserves to marry someone better.'

'I have never thought of marriage,' said Thambi, 'but I like you as you are, and you know it.'

'Aha! The cat is out of the bag,' said Shunya, 'so you love her. Thambi likes you as you are. You have no cancer. Now, will you do as I say?'

'Yes, Appa, you are everything to us.'

'Okay, listen. After ten days, Diana, you go back to England. You are not sick anymore. Check with your doctor. "Spontaneous remission," he will say, looking important, "happens sometimes."

'You then go back to work in the school. After six months, come back here. Then you and Thambi can get married and you can take him to England. Have a child and live happily.'

'But, Appa, why should I go away now?' protested Diana.

'You do as I say, otherwise don't speak to me. Go now, you golden-haired rabbit.'

'What do you say, Thambi?' she asked

'Whatever he says, if you are willing,' Thambi replied.

'Now,' said Shunya, 'a promise is a promise. No going back on it. Come here, let me bless you.' He placed his hands fondly on their bowed heads.

Unexpectedly, Diana kissed Shunya on his cheek, and giggling like a schoolgirl, ran away.

'Happy, happy, good, good,' said Shunya, and jumped around like a madman.

That night, Diana and Thambi met under the peepal tree near the temple pond. It was a full moon night. Frogs in love croaked their mating calls and twinkling fireflies danced in joy. Far away somewhere, a dog barked.

For the first time, they kissed each other, deeply in love.

Diana flew back to London soon after. The doctors declared her cured. 'Spontaneous remission,' they said echoing Shunya's words, 'sometimes happens'. She rejoined her old school and continued with her spiritual practice, which was very simple. She contemplated on Shunya's form for long periods every morning and before going to sleep, and felt as free and happy as the gentle breeze that blew in through her window on a lovely summer day.

The mail service between India and England was pretty slow in those days but she and Thambi kept in touch. She was waiting eagerly for the six-month period to get over so she could return and sit at Shunya's feet and go on those long walks in the coconut grove with her dear Thambi.

25

Not many days after Diana left for England, Prof. Bob Hawkins went back to the United States. Shunya had given him last-minute instructions on what he called 'how to approach the Great Void'. He was also told never to come back to India. No reasons were given. Bob kept in touch with Thambi by mail.

The congregations continued and there never was a dull day. One day, Shunya broke the camera of a documentary film-maker from Argentina, and on another day, he scolded the local headmaster in public for having an affair with his neighbour's wife. On yet another day, he brought back to normal a teenaged girl brought to him in chains, screaming, raving and frothing at the mouth, supposedly possessed by a demon, by slapping her sharply on both her cheeks and spitting into her mouth. And so, the drama went on.

Two months after Bob had left, a creature stranger than Shunya himself appeared. One of the general satsangs had just started when there was a commotion at the entrance. A bone-thin, dark, almost coal-black, gnome-like man, not more than five feet tall, hunch-backed, completely hairless and stark naked, was trying to get in, and the volunteers were trying their best to stop him.

'Catch him properly, he's slippery,' said one of them.

'No, no, you can't go in,' said another.

'*Glug gum gana, andi pundi, poolae,*' sang the creature.

'Can't make out a word,' said Sadasivan, who had just joined, 'maybe he is mad.'

'*Gudak bum, gudupudi,*' said the man to Sadasivan.

Shunya stood up and said loudly, 'Let him in.'

The volunteers let go. The strange man darted like an arrow in flight, and stood before Shunya.

'Guru Natha, oh my beloved Guru,' shouted Shunya, and they hugged each other. Then Shunya led him to his own seat under the jackfruit tree and sat at a respectable distance facing him.

In the shocked silence that had descended on the congregation, they conversed. No one else understood a word.

'*Gundi goppa mundi?*' said the Guru.

'*Gulu gulu goki china,*' said Shunya.

'*Tagara muthu, haggu khali, chichi,*' said the Guru.

'*Chitad phatti, googira,*' said Shunya.

Shunya stood up and said, 'Satsang over.' Holding the strange man's hand, he led him into the cottage.

'Thambi, you stay outside, until I call you.'

'Sadasiva, bring some food after an hour and knock on the door,' instructed Shunya, who then bolted it from the inside.

As the crowd dispersed, someone whispered, 'I think he is his Guru. You heard what he spoke? Some kind of ancient classical language, I think.'

'I think it is a mental disorder called glossolabia,' said Abraham, a young student of psychology quoting from his text book, 'meaningless words uttered in a rhythm during an attack of hysteria.'

Sadasivan went to get the food ready.

Thambi sat outside the cottage, waiting for Shunya to call him.

Sadasivan arrived with the food and knocked. The door opened and Shunya appeared. He took the fish curry and rice from Sadasivan. 'I have brought a bottle of toddy, Saami, for Guru Saami.'

'Yes, I can see. You can take it back. Guru Saami doesn't drink toddy. He is always as tight as a drunken owl. Thambi, you come in a little later.' He shut the door.

'Mysterious,' said Sadasivan, 'do you know what language Guru Saami spoke in?'

'No, but I think it is some kind of a private code language, something like the spoonerism you Keralites are famous for.'

'Anyway, you will have the chance to sleep near Guru Saami. You are a fortunate fellow.'

After an hour or so, Shunya opened the door and called Thambi in. 'Guru Saami has come all the way to initiate you,' he said, 'prostrate before him.'

Thambi prostrated, touching his head on the ground, and then stood up.

'*Pandi, pannada, uumbu,*' said Guru Saami, and gave Thambi a hard slap. Apparently satisfied, he rubbed his hands in glee, and walking behind him, landed a hard kick on his bum. Thambi fell down but wasn't hurt.

Thambi got up and looked towards Shunya. Shunya was sitting cross-legged on his rug and watching the whole show.

'*Poorum, poorum, vandhirum,*' said Guru Saami. Thambi suddenly realised that this time, the strange man was speaking Tamil. 'Enough, enough, it will come,' was what he had said.

'Prostrate again and go sleep,' came Shunya's voice.

Thambi prostrated once again, and this time, was rewarded with a soft massage on his head with the right hand, and some words he didn't understand. '*Pacchi, pacchi, bhalo, bhalo,*' said Guru Saami.

Thambi noticed that, although Guru Saami looked as though he hadn't had a bath in many years, there was no bad odour about him. Instead, a faint smell of jasmine filled the air. Thambi lay down on his mat. Guru Saami kept walking around in circles, uttering what Thambi thought were meaningless words. Shunya sat on his rug as usual and seemed unconcerned about what was happening. Thambi turned this way and that, trying to get some sleep.

Guru Saami stopped his gyrations and suddenly uttered a piercing, hair-raising shriek, frightening enough for Thambi to lunge for the door. As Thambi ran, Guru Saami stretched out his leg and tripped him.

Thambi fell, or rather his body fell flat on the floor of the cottage. Something snapped with a flash inside his head and he found himself released from the physical body, effortlessly penetrating the closed door and floating about outside in the courtyard. The whole experience was one of freedom and weightlessness. When he jotted down his experience later in his notebook, he likened it to how he thought the new butterfly feels when it breaks out of the cocoon, finds its wings and discovers an entirely new world. Looking around he noticed that the courtyard was deserted. The flourescent light above the night watchman's cubicle was lit. The watchman Dorai was fast asleep.

Thambi thought that he had died. He had suffered a serious injury while falling and now his soul was hovering outside. An irresistible desire to see his body possessed him, and instantaneously he found himself inside the cottage, looking at his own body lying prostrate on the ground. He had never looked at himself before like that. Ah! This is how you look, Thambi, he told himself. Strangely, there was no panic. Everything was so peaceful. Guru Saami continued going around in circles shouting something. Shunya still sat on the mat, his head turned towards the roof. Thambi felt that Shunya could see his soul floating near the roof. What Shunya did next confirmed his belief. In a deep voice, he said, 'Come back Thambi, enough for today.'

He felt that he was being tugged hard from below, and instantaneously, found himself back in the body. The first thing he noted was an almost painful heaviness as if he was clothed in lead. Guru Saami was kneeling beside him. Shunya whispered, 'Now, sleep.'

Thambi turned on his side obediently. Guru Saami resumed his merry-go-round. Thambi fell asleep and dreamt that he was a butterfly, flying high up among the treetops.

∾

In the morning, when he woke up, Thambi found the door open and Guru Saami missing.

'He is gone,' said Shunya, 'came for a purpose. From nothingness to nothingness.'

As they took their usual morning walk in the coconut grove, Shunya said, 'Guru Saami cannot be defined. Shunya met him in an old-fashioned home for the mentally challenged. He was waiting for Shunya. He was chained to a pillar. He smiled, looked at Shunya, broke the chains, iron, platinum, gold, all chains, and took Shunya into the open countryside.

'Cows mooed, goats bleated, little piglets played in the sunshine, the slender stream danced along, humming to itself, celebrating its freedom.

"See that freedom," said Guru Saami to Shunya,

"madness and freedom. You are nothing, Shunya, nothing to lose, nothing to gain. Be free."

'Guru Saami pointed at the building that they had escaped from and said, "We are mad, they are also mad in there. The only difference is that they are inside and we are outside. Got it?"

'Since then Shunya has been mad. Don't ask questions about Guru Saami, okay?'

After a while Thambi asked, 'Can I ask about my experience? I think I came out of my body and consciously moved about.'

'Happens, Thambi, happens. It is child's play. Ask no more questions.'

26

The satsangs went on as usual. Many more people came. A matted-haired sadhu from the Himalayas arrived with his numerous disciples. An interesting dialogue ensued.

'I came,' said the sadhu, 'because I felt a powerful force emanating from this direction, Saamiji. Who are you, really?'

'Shunya, nothing,' said Shunya.

'I understand. It is futile to repeat that question. You have merged with the Great Void, the original. We are trying to get there.'

'O matted-haired yogi,' said Shunya, 'you are almost there. The main obstacle now is your monastery in the Himalayas and your ever-increasing brood of disciples.

'Listen to the story of Naraga Asura, the chief of the demons. Once, they say, Naraga Asura and a dear friend of his went for a walk in the woods. Naraga suddenly bent down, picked up a shiny object from the earth and quickly popped it into the pocket of his dark jacket.

'"What have you picked up?" asked his friend

'"Oh! The wretched truth, satya; that which shines and dispels the darkness of ignorance," said Naraga.

'"In which case you are doomed," said the friend, "for you are the embodiment of darkness and ignorance."

'"Don't you worry, my friend," said Naraga Asura with a wicked wink, "I'll organise it. I'll organise it so perfectly and densely that the light won't have a single chance to show through."'

'Oh great yogi,' said Shunya, 'do you understand?

Break free of your establishment, or you'll never earn the freedom you seek.

'Prestige, power, name and fame have to go. Attachment comes in many guises, some hardly recognisable. Get rid of it all and be free.

'Listen to the story of the monk who got himself a cat. In a small hut, under a peepal tree beside the river Ganga, lived an ascetic whose only possessions were a small copper water pot and two pairs of kaupins, narrow strips of coarse cloth, same as the one you are wearing, to protect and cover Cupid's arrow and the creative spheroids that hang from the tree of life in the middle of the Garden of Eden—the forbidden fruit.

'One momentous day, a field rat chewed up one of the kaupins he had washed and hung on the clothes line to dry. Being a firm believer in non-violence, he refused to trap or kill the rat. Since he was also kind-hearted, he decided to provide food to a hungry cat. So he acquired a cat. The cat needed milk, so he begged someone for a cow. To milk and look after the cow, he found a young girl. And before he knew it, he had married her. Children were born, and being married, he was not entitled to beg like a holy beggar. To provide for his family, he had to abandon his peaceful solitude and go to the city to find a job. The city swallowed him up.

'So be careful. The snare creeps in imperceptibly. Keep life free. Don't let the cat get in. Be free and run from all establishments.'

After the satsang, the sadhu sent his disciples away. Shunya sat under the jackfruit tree with the sadhu who prepared his pipe to smoke hemp. Just before he lit his pipe, Shunya said, 'Now wait a minute, oh yogi, shall I teach you how to get high without your hemp?'

'I tried for many years,' said the sadhu, 'but I found very little success with pranayama, if that's what you are talking about…'

'No, no, breathing in and breathing out very fast, or hyperventilation,' said Shunya, 'starves your brain of fresh air, and gives you a gentle floating sensation. More carbon dioxide and less oxygen may even result in elaborate hallucinations of light and music, but what you'll experience now is different.'

Saying that, Shunya let out a mad, shrill laugh, almost like a scream. Standing up with his eyes closed, he stretched his right foot and firmly pressed his big toe on the sadhu's forehead.

'What are you doing?' shouted the sadhu, his body trembling, 'The world around me is crumbling and vanishing in a flood of brilliant light. My hair is standing on end with ecstasy. Every cell is filled with bliss. Oh! Here goes even me, the petty me. The giant wave of light has washed everything away. I am everywhere, you are me, that jackfruit is me…words fail, I…'

He became silent. On his face was an ecstatic smile. Copious tears of joy flowed down the corners of his eyes and drenched his chest.

After a while, Shunya stroked him on his neck with his right hand and said, 'Come back, come back.'

Slowly, reluctantly, the sadhu opened his eyes. Seeing Shunya sitting before him, he prostrated himself at his feet and stood up. 'Thank you for your grace. I now understand. You are the Great Void, so am I. Now I shall wander the earth in freedom.'

Laying his hand on his head, Shunya blessed him and said, 'Roam the earth like a lion now. You are free. There is nothing but Shunya. Go now and don't linger.'

Taking leave of his disciples, the sadhu became a solitary wanderer. He never went back to the monastery of which he was the head. Free as the wind, he walked the earth, absorbed in the joy of Shunya, the Great Void. His disciples went on a pilgrimage to Rameswaram and returned home without the master.

Eventually, the seniormost among them became the head of the large ashram.

27

One evening at a general satsang, a saffron-robed, tonsured monk of the Dasanami order of Sanyasis arrived accompanied by a powerful politician, a minister, who was one of his disciples.

The monk claimed that he was a great scholar of Vedanta and though originally from Kerala, he was presently the head of a grand monastery in the holy city of Benares. He claimed to have thousands of disciples including many from the West. He was striking to look at—tall, well-built, fair and handsome.

Shunya took one look at him and said, 'Fraud, kallan, this fellow stole his wife's jewellery and ran away. He killed his wife. She died of shock.' The monk went red in the face.

'I am C. Gopalan, a minister, and Swamiji is my guru,' said the politician, trying to interrupt.

'Birds of the same feather,' said Shunya

'I would like to ask you a few questions,' said the monk imperiously.

'Ask.'

'Who was the founder of the order of the Dasanami order of Sanyasis?'

'Neither your ancestor, nor mine. Ask useful questions.'

'All right. Who is your guru, what is your spiritual lineage, and what authority do you claim?' asked the monk angrily.

'Sure, I don't have ministerial authority,' said Shunya. Some of the people present began to snigger.

'You are a con man and a cheat,' said the monk, 'You have no scriptural authority. People like you should be jailed.'

Kunjan Namboodiri, who was present among the gathering, stood up and said, 'I protest. You can't say that to Saami. If you need to discuss Vedanta, come, I am ready to meet you anywhere, anytime. Saami is my Guru and I affirm that he is the living embodiment of Vedanta.'

The monk was silenced. Seething, he stood up and walked out of the place with the minister in tow. 'I'll take care of the fellow,' muttered the politician as he followed his guru.

'Kunjan Namboodiri, great scholar of Vedanta, please sit down,' said Shunya. 'Now that the great guru has left, I'll tell you the story of a real guru.'

'Long, long ago, in the Middle East, there lived a businessman who, since his childhood, evinced great interest in matters of the spirit. But having been born poor and having experienced the deprivation extreme poverty brings, he also developed the desire to be free of it. So, he spent the greater part of his life trying to become rich. In the process, he neglected his spiritual aspirations.

'When he reached the age of fifty-five, he realised that he had attained the highest level of happiness that money could buy and yet there was something missing. He had all the riches in the world but he found that he was poor in spirit. He no longer felt satisfied with anything in this world. The flame of spiritual longing, which had been on the verge of being snuffed out, was rekindled. Being a practical man, he took concrete steps.

'He gave away his business empire to his children,

and built himself a little cottage near an oasis, far from his old home, and went to live there, so he could fully immerse himself in the search of the spirit. He took with him all the religious and philosophical treatises he had gathered over the years, determined to study them in depth, undisturbed by the world outside.

'At the right moment, he found a new cook who was willing to live in the oasis, and he took him along so that he could pursue his studies and meditations uninterruptedly.

'He lived that way for eight years, studying, meditating, and eating the simple food prepared by his cook.

'At the end of eight years, he realised that what he was seeking could not be found without the help of a teacher, a guru who had walked the path and found the Truth.

'So he told his cook to take care of the house until he returned, and he set out into the great desert, hoping to find a murshid, a guru, in one of the many caves that dotted the landscape. He had heard that highly advanced hermits lived in some of those caves.

'For many days he searched, until one morning, he came upon a venerable-looking hermit with a flowing white beard, who looked like a biblical prophet.

'"Sir," he said to the hermit, "I feel, deep down in my heart, that you are a great sage. Kindly accept me as your disciple!"

'"All that is fine, you look like a sincere soul," said the hermit, "but I have a problem. I cannot accept a disciple without permission from my own master."

'"Then please ask him and accept me," said the seeker.

'"That is precisely the problem," said the hermit, "my master has disappeared. The last I heard of him, he was living in a cottage in an oasis, cooking for a businessman-turned-seeker. I am actually looking for him, and when I find him, I'll seek permission and then accept you."

"'Now, wait a minute," said the seeker, "I am myself a businessman-turned-seeker who lives in a cottage in an oasis not far away. I have a cook too. By any chance, could it be that...no, no, it can't be. Can you please describe him?"

'When he heard the description, the seeker's hair stood on end. "Come," he said to the hermit, "let's go to my cottage."

'When they arrived, the diminutive, nondescript cook came out to welcome them. The prophet-like hermit bowed low and said, "Master, you were here for eight years with this man. Surely you would have worked your way on him!"

"'Yes," said the great master, "it took me eight years to make him understand that he needed a teacher. Now you take care of him. I have more work to do somewhere else."

'With that, the master, who was also the master cook who knew the right ingredients, walked out of the cottage and disappeared into...okay, you tell me.'

'Nothingness,' said Thambi.

'Aha! Kunjan, did you hear that? Sada, did you hear that? All of you heard? Thambi is growing up.'

'Saami,' said Kunjan Namboodiri, 'what a beautiful story.'

'Yes, yes, beautiful story all right, but let it register clearly. Time is running out, the timeless is around the corner. Stay empty. Satsang is over. Everybody, go.'

Everyone dispersed.

༄

That night, the police raided Shunya's cottage but couldn't discover the incriminating evidence they were hoping to find. After the raid, the minister got a call from Inspector Chandu Nair, who was in charge of the operation.

'What happened?' asked the politician.

'Nothing, sir. I think I messed it up.'

'Idiot! I asked you to take a packet of hemp with you, plant it there, and pretend that you found it.'

'I did, sir, although I still feel guilty about it but I think I took the wrong packet. It turned out to be the packet of toffees that I had bought for my son's birthday. Can't figure out how that could have happened.'

'Stupid fool,' shouted the politician angrily, 'no wonder the police department is so ineffective these days! See me tomorrow.'

The inspector went back home puzzled and upset. He asked his wife before going to bed, 'Did you see a brown paper packet on the table?'

'Yes,' she said, 'I opened it.'

The inspector thought she was giving him a strange look. His heart sank. 'And?' he asked.

'It was full of toffees, so I put it in a safe place,' she said smiling. 'Too many ants these days. Sunny was waiting to thank you for it, but I think he was too tired and fell asleep. Why are you so late today?'

'Official work,' said the inspector, 'there was an emergency.'

Before going to bed, he checked the brown paper packet. Sure enough, it was full of toffees; there was no sign of hemp.

That night, Inspector Chandu stayed awake.

28

A few nights after the raid, Shunya woke Thambi up around midnight and said, 'Come here and sit down.'

They sat facing each other. Shunya asked, 'Thambi, are you afraid of me?'

'No, Saami.'

'Afraid of anything else?'

'No, Saami.'

'No fear?'

'No, Saami.'

'You have conquered fear?'

'I don't know but I am not afraid.'

'All right, come with me.'

The half-moon shed sufficient light on the path. Shunya led Thambi through the coconut grove, past the temple pond, across paddy fields and an areca nut garden, and over a small hillock. The fact that they were approaching a crematorium was evident from the strong odour of burning flesh.

It was a traditional Hindu crematorium, not an electric one. Dead bodies were burnt over a pile of logs in the open. 'I think we have reached the cremation grounds,' Thambi said.

'Yes, here we are. See, everybody has left. The body is reduced to ashes, bhasmam. The relatives have taken the last thing they could—a pot full of ashes, as remembrance, to satisfy themselves. The skull is cracking with a loud bang, the final fart. Ashes to ashes, beautiful, beautiful.

'Now, you meditate here, near this half-burnt body of

the young girl that was brought in this evening. Close your eyes and visualise the wrathful black goddess of the dark night: she with the red, blood-dripping, lolling tongue and rolling eyes, wearing a garland of skulls round her neck, a skirt of severed arms around her naked waist, with one of her four arms holding a bloody, just decapitated head, and the other a lethal sword. Meditate on the dark lady of the night who lives in the cremation grounds, and has jackals for companions.

'Chant continuously, *krim, hrim, Kalika, phat, phat*, and don't open your eyes no matter what happens, until you hear my voice. I am going now, but I shall be back when required. Start! No questions. If you open your eyes, you are dead.' Saying this, Shunya slipped away, and vanished behind the hillock.

The crematorium was in a little valley, surrounded by hills and thick vegetation. Thambi found himself all alone. In the moonlight, he could discern the still smouldering body of someone who must have been a beautiful lady at one time. The stench was nauseating.

Scared but fighting the desire to flee, Thambi sat down cross-legged at the place pointed out by Shunya, close to what was left of the corpse. Closing his eyes, he started to chant.

'*Krim, hrim, Kalika, phat, phat.*'

Far away, a jackal howled. The fear of the unknown held him in its vice-like grip. Never before had he felt so terrified. He found himself trembling and sweating profusely.

Dogs began to bark and packs of jackals howled. The howls were drawing closer. The wind grew stronger and it began to howl too. It was as if a cyclone was setting in. The ground shook under him, dust and ashes twirled around his body, but Thambi resisted the temptation to open his eyes.

Slowly, the wind subsided and the ground stopped quaking. The jackals continued to howl at intervals. Finally, the howling stopped too, and an eerie silence fell, only to be broken by the sound of jingling anklets, as though a female dancer was heading that way.

The next moment, he heard a blood-curdling shriek that turned into a horrendous cackling laughter that set him shivering uncontrollably, but he continued to chant the mantra and keep his eyes shut.

'Open your eyes,' shrieked the presence. Thambi kept chanting.

'I have your long-departed relatives with me. Here, look, your father and your mother. Don't you want to see your dear mother?' The voice had now become soft and inviting. A warm hand touched his chin, and he heard his mother's voice, 'Look, my darling, don't you want to see me, your dear mother?' The stench was now replaced by a sweet, intoxicating scent, but Thambi clenched his jaws and wept. He opened them only after Shunya called out to him.

He heard the familiar voice say, 'Have no fear, you have passed the test. Open your eyes.'

Still frightened, Thambi opened his eyes slowly and carefully. There was no one except Shunya sitting beside him.

'Now pick a little ash from here and apply it to your forehead,' said Shunya, 'Shiva loves ashes, Shiva the Lord of the cremation grounds. Love death and embrace it, for it's your constant companion.'

Thambi applied the ash to his forehead. Shunya asked, 'Are you okay?'

'Yes, Saami.'

'Then let's go.'

As they came back to the cottage, the faint pre-dawn light was colouring the sky.

'You can sleep till noon,' said Shunya, 'No asanas, no meditation, no walks, nothing. Sleep, you have been awake all night.'

Thambi fell asleep and woke up at noon. He didn't find Shunya in the cottage. He washed and went to the toddy shop to meet Sadasivan. He met him near the door.

'I was coming to enquire about what had happened,' said Sadasivan. 'The cottage door was closed when I came to see you. I waited for an hour and then left.'

'Did you see Saami?'

'No.'

'He is not in the cottage. He must have quietly slipped out when no one was looking and gone into the forest. I must tell you what happened yesterday. Saami won't mind if I tell you. In any case, he didn't prohibit me from telling anyone.'

'Wait,' said Sadasivan, 'let's go home. Actually I was coming to invite you. Bhavani asked me to. Her mother is visiting and she is a good cook. She has made ada pradhaman. Come. The old lady also wanted to talk to you. She knows a lot about occult matters. In the evening, I'll take her to the general satsang to meet Saami.'

'Okay, if you say so,' said Thambi, and walked with Sadasivan to his house.

The local tailor, Bhasi, seeing Thambi pass by, said to his assistant, 'Unnh! He has put on some weight, this

Tamil fellow. Sada-annan must be feeding him well, or is it sister Bhavani?'

After a sumptuous lunch served by Bhavani, they sat on the verandah, chewing betel leaf and talking.

Thambi told them the story of the previous night in detail. When he had finished, Sadasivan said, 'In the early days, Saami also showed me something strange and mysterious. I haven't told anyone, not even Bhavani, but now I think I should share it. Maybe it should go into the notes Saami asked you to keep.

'One night, as I was shutting the bar and getting ready to go home, Saami asked me to come with him. It was about 11.30 p.m. In those days, there were no crowds. Hardly anyone knew him. It was a dark night and I took a torch with me.

'He took me through the coconut grove, the paddy fields and the arecanut groves, over the hillock and across the crematorium ground you mentioned, until we entered a densely wooded area. Not a word was spoken till then. I was, of course, a little scared as I still thought that he was mentally unstable.

'After we had pushed our way through the thick and thorny vegetation for a few minutes, he put his finger to his lips and whispered, "Shh! Don't make a noise. It's dangerous. Look there."

'In a clearing, not far from where we were hidden, was a fairly large pond. Beautiful damsels, stark naked, were swimming and generally frolicking in the pond, teasing each other and spraying water. A lovely scent of jasmine saturated the air. It was so intoxicating that I lost control, forgot everything and exclaimed loudly, "Aha!"

'Saami slapped his palm on my face to keep me quiet.

The heavenly ladies stopped their games, looked around suspiciously and just vanished into thin air.

'After waiting motionlessly for a few minutes, we wended our way back. "Yakshis. You are lucky they didn't attack you," was all that Saami said, when I asked him for an explanation. To this day, I don't know what it was and didn't dare to go there alone at night. During the day, there is nothing there. Just an ordinary pond but people don't frequent it because it is a watering hole for wild animals.'

'He was right. You were lucky,' said Kamalamma, Bhavani's mother, 'they must have been Yakshis. They are female spirits who haunt forests, ponds and caves in remote areas and are known to be experts in dance and music. Some of them are very powerful, and some very wise. My father used to tell me that Yakshis, using their magical powers, transform themselves into beautiful women, wearing pure white. They would wait for lonely travellers who passed through remote, thickly forested areas in the olden days. They attracted the travellers with the strong smell of jasmine which they exuded, and their seductive voices, and lured them into having sex with them.

'Once the men fell for their charms, they suddenly reverted to their original tall, ugly-looking forms, tore open the men's abdomens with their claws and long canines, and feasted on their intestines.

'My Guru says they still exist and the only way to escape is not to be attracted to beautiful women in solitary places. If, by chance, it happens, you have to shout *Bhairavi, Bhairavi*, the name of the great Goddess. Yakshis disappear the moment they hear the holy name.'

Bhavani said, 'Amma knows all these stories, Thambi,

you'll get bored! She knows so many of them. She herself claims to be an amateur magician, and has a Guru too.'

'No, no,' protested Thambi, 'I like these stories. My grandmother too knew many.'

'Not stories, Bhavani, they are true. Don't you believe what Sadasiva said? They are true. Ask your Saami if you get a chance. If you are busy, I'll tell you some other day.'

'I am not busy,' said Thambi, not wanting to hurt her feelings, 'tell me some more.'

'See, he is a good boy,' said Kamalamma, 'I'll tell you a short one about Kutti-chathan. Have you heard of Kutti-chathan?'

'Not really.'

'Then listen. 'Kutti' means, as you know, a small child. 'Chathan' means spirit, not like Satan that the Christians talk about, but mischievous little spirits who love to play pranks. They are more like monkeys and are usually in the form of three-year-old boys.

'Great magicians bring these kutti-chathans under their control and use them to perform wonders, and sometimes trouble their enemies.

'Muttakaad Srikandan Namboodiri had a chathan under his control. He used to perform wonders like producing flowers from nowhere, making valuable jewellery from hidden treasures appear mysteriously, and so on. "Kutti-chathan, bring me this, or bring me that," was all that he had to say.

'Once, he punished a rival Namboodiri, who tried to kill him using black magic, by sending his kutti-chathan to trouble him.

'When that Namboodiri sat down to eat, the food in front of him would become excreta. Every now and then, the roof of his house would catch fire. His wife complained of the constant stench that seemed to come from his body. Not being able to bear the agony of it all, the man jumped into a pond and committed suicide.

'They say, Srikandan Namboodiri died a terrible death because the kutti-chathan turned against him. Some say it was the rival's curse. Anyhow, he died in great pain with open sores all over his body. Even his eyes were not spared. The great Karinkunna Siddhan, who I consider my Guru, managed to acquire all the rare palm-leaf manuscripts on magic and incantations which Srikandan Namboodiri had hidden away before he died, and...'

'Amma, Thambi has to go and rest. He must be tired,' said Sadasivan.

'Yes, yes, go and rest my son, just five minutes, let me complete.'

'Please do,' said Thambi.

'Yeah, so as I was saying, my Guru found all those works on magic. One of them, which he let me look at, describes how a kutti-chathan can be brought under one's control.

'On a full moon day, especially on a Saturday, find a large peepal tree that grows close to the bank of a river. Climb up the tree, and sitting on a branch from where you can see the river, wait patiently. Keep chanting to yourself, "*Kuttichatavaishyavaishya, aakarshaya, ha ha, ho ho, chooth.*"

'After a while, you will see a tiny, baby-like kutti-chathan coming to take his bath wearing only a small konam, the yellow triangular g-string. Wait till he removes the konam, puts it under the tree, and plunges into the river naked to have his bath, as kutti-chathans always do.

'Slip down quietly, and seizing the konam, climb up again and wait patiently.

'Soon, having finished his bath, the kutti-chathan will emerge from the waters. Finding his underwear missing, he will start looking for it as chathans hate to be seen naked.

'Then, you call down from your perch on the tree and say, "Chathan, I have got your konam here. I'll give it to you only if you obey me and become my slave." He'll plead with you, beg you to spare him, and so on, but you must not give in.

'At last, he'll agree, and make a covenant with you. Some simple condition like you have to set aside some special food for him every day under the jackfruit tree, or some such thing.

'That's it. He'll remain your slave, and you can work wonders with him. Only, don't forget the covenant. If you do, he can turn against you and destroy you.

'Now then, have you heard of the changali madan?'

'I think I'll have to go now,' said Thambi, 'Saami may be looking for me. Amma, I'll come some other time. Your stories are very interesting.'

'Listen, son, there is something I wanted to ask you. My Guru wishes to see your Saami. Can you fix up an appointment for him?'

'Amma, Saami gets very upset with recommendations. I wouldn't dare to, normally, but I'll try.'

Thambi thanked everyone and drove back with Sadasivan in his Fiat Elegant. The cottage door was closed. 'Saami just came back,' one of the volunteers said.

Thambi and Sadasivan waited outside for Shunya to come out, eat and get ready for the satsang. There was still one hour left.

Shunya called out to Thambi from inside the cottage. Thambi ran to the door and said, 'I am here, Saami, and so is Sada annan.'

Shunya came out and sat under the jackfruit tree. Sadasivan brought him his food. 'So what did Kamalamma say?' he asked while eating his meal.

'She knew many stories,' Thambi said, 'and when I was about to leave, she wanted to know if her guru could see you.'

'Karrinkunna Siddhan, umph, he wants to challenge me, not just see me. Good opportunity. Send word that he can see me next Tuesday. Sadasiva, you tell that to your mother-in-law. Ah! Lovely tapioca today, quite fresh!'

At seven o'clock, Shunya was ready for the gathering. There were about a hundred people, from the north, south, east and west, rich and poor, learned and unlearned. To Shunya, it made no difference.

'Aiyo! Meenakshi has come,' he said, and laughed loudly. 'When is the baby coming out?'

'Next month,' said Salim, her husband. 'We have come here for your blessings.'

'Blessings from Shunyam, nothing from nothing, ha ha!' said Shunya. Then his eyes fell on Meenakshi's uncle, M.K. Nair.

'Aaah! M.K! Good man, you look troubled. See me tomorrow at 10 a.m.'

'Okay, Saami,' said M.K.

'Appointment with nothing, you wanted it, you got it. M.K. meets nothing, good headlines for newspapers. "Nothing" is popular these days.'

Eapen, a Christian rubber planter, who was seventy years old, said, 'Saami, Jesus must have been like you, unconventional and unpredictable. All simplicity has vanished now. Only ceremonies and masses and medieval robes remain. They speak in the name of God, but do they know God? Is God their brother-in-law?'

'Blessed are the pure in heart, for they shall see God,' said Shunya, quoting the New Testament, 'blessed are the pure in heart, Hindu, Christian, Sikh, Muslim. Pure in heart, clean heart, vacuum, nothing inside, empty to receive nothingness. God, dog, both are the same nothingness. Blessed are the empty-hearted, for they shall know nothingness. But Eapen, watch out, don't talk like me, they won't like what you say. Shunya knows nothing.'

Thangamma, a pretty young prostitute from the brothel in the neighbourhood, came to see Shunya out of curiosity. This was her first visit. She sat far away from the rest of the crowd, right at the end of the courtyard. Shunya's eyes rested on her for a moment. 'What is your name?' he asked.

'Who? Me? Thangamma.'

'Thangamma, come here and sit in front of me.'

Thangamma stood up and looked around, wondering what to do. Most people of the locality knew who she was.

'You,' said Shunya firmly, 'I asked you to come here. Come!'

Thangamma gathered courage and walked up to him.

'Now, sit down.' Shunya stretched his right leg and put his foot in front of her. 'Massage my feet, my dear daughter, I have a bad pain there. Come on.'

Thangamma started massaging his feet. Halfway through, she broke down and started weeping loudly.

'Don't cry, don't cry,' said Shunya tenderly, stroking her head and kissing her cheeks, 'how sweet is your massage, so full of devotion. You have such a pretty face, you could have been a film star. It's a pity that a film producer hasn't set his eyes on you.'

The scene was so touching that many others shed tears on that day, but there were some who were jealous and angry.

'That's enough,' said Shunya to Thangamma, 'go home, daughter. 'Satsang is over,' he announced, 'everyone can go.'

Thangamma met Bhavani before returning home. She said, 'Bhavani amma, I believe you have Saami's photograph with you. Can I have a copy? Please, I beg you. He is God himself.'

'I'll ask my husband,' said Bhavani, feeling slightly jealous.

A few days later later, Thangamma procured Shunya's photograph from Bhavani, got it framed, and kept it safely inside her tiny tin trunk. Every morning, as soon as she woke up, and every evening, before she went to sleep, she kissed the photograph, bowed down to it, and put it back in the trunk. A month after she had started this practice, a rich and distinguished-looking client arrived. Looking at the girls who were paraded before him, he chose Thangamma, and paid Madhavi-akkan, who ran the brothel, a large sum of money so that he could be with Thangamma all night.

After the initial two rounds of sex, and three large pegs of XXX rum, he got her to pose for him, sitting down, lying on the bed, looking out of the window, and so on. Then he examined her eyes, her lips and her hair, as if he was sampling a product for sale. Before she could ask him if he was crazy or just joking, he said, 'Thangam, you are truly Thangam, pure gold. Will you think I am a liar if I tell you that I am a film producer, and that I am looking for a fresh heroine for my new film?'

'No, why should I?' said Thangamma.

'But suppose I say that you seem to be the perfect choice and offer you the role?'

'Sir,' said Thangamma, 'please don't talk rot. You men have no right to play with the lives of young girls. I have already been a victim of such tall promises. A young man from Madras made me run away from home, promising to make me a film star. Where am I today at the age of eighteen? Working in a brothel, having sex with unknown men, just to earn my livelihood. I don't believe anybody anymore. So, have your sex, and go your way, and don't waste your precious time. Where do you want it this time? Front or back?'

'Great,' said the man, whose name was Jose, 'You even speak like a heroine. What a dialogue that was. Let me assure you, my dear girl, I am not trying to take you for a ride. I think you have the potential to become a big star. It's your life, do what you want, but remember, such opportunities don't knock on your door always.'

That was when she suddenly remembered Shunya's words, 'You could have been a film star...' 'Just a minute,' she said to Jose, and opening her tin trunk, looked inside at the photograph of Shunya. 'Saami, please help, I don't know what to do,' she prayed silently. She thought she heard Shunya say, 'Go, child, go,' or maybe it was her imagination. In any case, she decided to take the risk. She had always been a risk-taker.

'Okay,' she said, shutting the trunk, 'but how are you going to convince Madhavi-akkan? I am not going to run away without asking her.'

'Leave that to me,' said Jose, 'and to prove that I am a decent man, I won't trouble you anymore tonight. It's quite late already. You sleep now, you sweet thing. I'll talk to your akkan tomorrow morning.'

Saying that, Jose stretched himself out on one side of the bed, and gestured to Thangamma to sleep beside him. They slept soundly.

❧

The next morning, after haggling about the price, Madhavi finally settled for five thousand rupees. 'You must be really serious if you are paying so much money,' she said. 'Tell me, what are you going to do with her? Marry her, or make a high-class call-girl out of her?'

'I haven't decided,' said Jose, 'but I am sure you don't care either way.'

'Really, I don't,' said Madhavi, kissing the wad of hundred-rupee notes in her hand. 'Thangam, don't forget akkan, okay. I gave you refuge when you had none.'

'I am grateful to you, akkan,' said Thangamma, touching her feet. Then she took out her tin trunk, which had the only precious thing she possessed, and nodded to Jose.

'May Lord Guruvayurappan bless you,' said Madhavi.

On that note, they left in a taxi which Jose had hired. Three of her colleagues were there to bid her farewell.

❧

They travelled by train to Madras, where Jose put her up in a hotel in Kodambakkam, where most of the cine studios were located. For the first few days, he allowed her to rest. Then began the rehearsals and the training. Her first movie was about a village lass who comes to the city to become a film star, only to end up in a brothel, until she is rescued by a kind man.

Jose was right. She was indeed a natural actress, and the film was a hit. Jose gave her a new name, Chaaya, which meant shade.

Chaaya acted in many movies, and in a short time, went on to become a super-star. Jose and she remained close friends, but their relationship was mainly professional. In her sprawling bungalow, she had a beautiful shrine in which were only two deities. One was a small icon of Jesus Christ carrying the cross, and the other was Shunya Saami. His photograph, framed in gold, was placed on a silver pedestal. She prayed in front of it daily and lit incense.

One hot summer day, Chaaya, as she sat in her study, going through the script of her next movie, was suddenly filled with this overwhelming desire to meet her Saami. The longing to visit his abode as quickly as possible became irresistible. Swiftly, she finalised her travel arrangements. She was to fly the next day to Thiruvananthapuram, but it was not to be.

That night, a massive fire broke out, and her house was practically gutted. The fire was attributed variously to a short circuit in the wiring, inter-star rivalry, and black magic activated by professional jealousy. But whatever it was, Chaaya was no more.

When Jose walked in with the police inspector the next morning, he found Chaaya lying dead in her shrine. Her burns were not too serious. Asphyxiation seemed to be the cause of her death. She had died holding the photograph of her Saami close to her heart. And even in death, she had a beautiful smile on her lips. Her Saami was with her forever; rather, she had reached his abode or so it seemed.

Jose first thought that he would seek permission from the police and keep the picture in his own bedroom, but in the end decided to let her keep what was so dear to her. Jose had wanted a Christian burial for her but the Church refused on the grounds that she was not a Christian and so the photograph was cremated along with her body according to Hindu rites.

The news of Chaaya's death was in all the newspapers. Sadasivan brought it to Shunya's notice. He merely smiled and said, 'Now she is free, my little Thangam, gold. She is in the real abode of Shunya, the Zero-Land. Be happy, Sadasiva.'

Sadasivan wiped his tears and went home.

29

The morning after Thangamma's first and only meeting with Shunya, Thambi led M.K. to his presence.

'M.K. looks so worried,' said Shunya, and clapped his hands.

'Saami, I am worried about you,' said M.K., coming straight to the point, 'you may be a crazy guy, but you are a good fellow and mean no harm. Unfortunately, there are people, powerful people, mind you, who hate you for various reasons and wouldn't hesitate to eliminate you. I have definite and reliable information on this.

'Maybe they are plain jealous, or feel threatened by your unconventional ways. For instance, many still feel that Meenakshi, my niece, married Salim because you encouraged her.

'I won't go into details, but anger and hate seem to be simmering beneath the surface. Can't say when it will erupt. I don't think that your old cottage caught fire by accident. Worse things can happen.

'What I wanted to suggest is this. I'll get two boys from the Communist Party cadre, who are very faithful to me, to be your personal bodyguards. They are trained in the martial art of Kalaripayattu. They will be with you constantly. Actually, I myself can't figure out why I am so concerned about you. Sometimes, I think you are raving mad.'

Shunya burst into loud laughter. 'Protection for nothingness,' he said between peals of laughter, 'bodyguards for the Shunya. Whoever heard of that? I bow to you a thousand times, M.K., but no, no, no, no security, no bodyguards, let Shunya be free. You are a good fellow. Don't worry.'

'Okay,' said M.K., standing up, 'I said what I thought was right. I leave it to you. I have warned you and that's it. Thambi, let me know if your Saami changes his mind. I have to go now.' M.K. walked away in a huff.

'Protection for Shunya, bodyguards for nobody,' Shunya kept repeating, as he went into the cottage and shut the door.

Thambi discussed what had happened with Sadasivan and Bhavani. 'What do we do?' asked Sadasivan.

'I don't know,' said Thambi, 'but surely Saami will not allow any such thing. The other day he was mad at me because the two men whom you engaged were following him everywhere. He threatened to run away to an unknown place.'

'I think we should try to persuade Saami,' said Sadasivan.

'If you ask me,' said Bhavani, 'Saami needs no protection. He himself is the protector of all.'

There the matter ended for the time being.

30

The next Tuesday, Karinkunna Siddhan, the great master of Tantra, and a reputedly powerful magician, arrived at around 10 a.m. Thambi had sent word to Bhavani's mother, Kamalamma, that Shunya was willing to see him in the evening. He had turned up at the wrong time. Siddhan was accompanied by two of his disciples, a fair, nondescript man, and a ravishing woman with thick, black hair that almost reached her knees.

Siddhan himself looked weird with his matted hair and flowing beard, along with the bright red, ankle-length silk robe, a rosary made of gooseberry-sized crystals around his neck, and gold rings studded with different kinds of precious stones on his fingers. His dark, deep-set eyes seemed to be on fire.

Ignoring the volunteer who tried to stop him, and pushing past Sadasivan and Thambi who were trying to reason with him, Siddhan rushed to the door of the cottage and banged on the door shouting, 'Come out, you fraud, you madman, I am waiting for you.'

The door opened and Shunya stepped out. 'Stop screaming,' he said, as cool as a watermelon, 'come and sit down here, under the jackfruit tree.'

'I do not propose to waste my time sitting here,' said Siddhan, still shouting, 'what arrogance to ask me to come here instead of you visiting me. That old hag got it all wrong. I have come now to say that I challenge you to display your powers, at a place that I choose. I'll display mine. Let's have a duel in magic. I'll defeat you and finish you off, and you'll be left with no option but to run away. What do you have to say to that?'

Shunya burst out laughing. 'Since you insist,' he said, 'I'll surely come, but don't blame me if you lose your balls in the process. What use would that sensuous nymph standing beside you be if you cannot raise the kundalini between your legs…'

'We'll see who does what and to whom,' sneered Siddhan. 'Tonight, at 12.30, come to the Karamana Kunnu. If you don't, I'll take it that you are afraid of accepting my challenge, and that you are a fake, and all your followers are liars. All of you heard what I said?'

Sadasivan went up to Siddhan and said angrily, 'You may be my mother-in-law's Guru, but another word from you against Saami, and I'll break your bones.'

'Cool down, Sadasiva,' said Shunya, 'I accept the challenge. Shunya will meet you at Karamana Kunnu tonight. Go now before I do something that you won't like.'

'Come,' said Siddhan to his disciples, 'let's not waste our time here,' and chanting loudly, '*brrum, mada mada, phat phat,*' turned abruptly and walked away, followed by his disciples.

'*Brrum, kada kada, cut cut,*' said Shunya, grinning widely, 'it's going to be very interesting tonight. Thambi and Sadasiva, both of you come with me.'

'Certainly,' said Sadasivan, 'I am going to take you in my car, Saami. The place is at least ten kilometres from here. Please don't say no.'

'Okay,' said Shunya, 'so be it. Thambi, bring with you a pot of water, three limes, a knife, a candle and a matchbox. We'll show this fellow our tricks. Be here at eleven, both of you.'

Shunya went into the cottage and shut the door. 'That Siddhan is a dangerous fellow,' said Sadasivan to Thambi, 'I am going to take my sickle along.'

'If you ask me,' said Thambi, 'there is no need to. Saami is capable of handling anything. I won't say that I am not scared, but I feel he can handle it. But it's a good idea to take a flashlight.'

'You are right,' said Sadasivan.

At eleven, Sadasivan and Thambi stood outside the cottage waiting for Shunya to open the door. At five past eleven, Shunya stepped out of the cottage, smiled, walked straight to Sadasivan's Fiat, sat in the back seat, and shut the door. 'Let's go,' he said.

With Sadasivan driving, and Thambi beside him in the front seat, they started out, bound for the Karamana Kunnu hill. At this time in the night, there was hardly any traffic, but as was his practice always, Sadasivan drove at a moderate speed.

'Karamana Kunnu, they say, is a dangerous place,' said Sadasivan. 'Even though it is just on the outskirts of the city, it is said that the place is infested with cobras, bats and jackals, and is a favourite haunt of evil spirits. I haven't been there, but my mother-in-law says that half way up the hillock, its mouth covered by thorny shrubs, is a small cave through which one enters a labrinyth of tunnels. The tunnels end in a large cave near the top of the hill, where Siddhan lives with his Yakshis and the ghoul known as kutti-chathan.'

'Shunya knows,' said Shunya, 'and Shunya also knows that Muttakad Srikandan Namboodiri, this fool Siddhan's Guru, who died a horrible death, was the grandson of the Namboodiri who challenged Father Kadamuttam and lost.'

'You mean the famous Kadamuttam?' asked Sadasivan.

'Yes, and don't ask anymore questions. Just drive.'

After a brief silence, Sadasivan asked Thambi in a low tone, 'Have you heard of Kadamuttam?'

'No,' whispered Thambi.

'He was a Christian priest who ventured into the thick forests of Tenmalai in search of cattle that had wandered off from his parish, and was captured by the tribals who were reputed to be powerful sorcerers. The story goes that they were also cannibals, and were on the verge of sacrificing him to their black goddess, when he was saved by their chief's daughter who had fallen in love with him at first sight.

'Her father, the chief, having agreed to the match, taught Kadamuttam all the secrets of sorcery. Kadamuttam pretended to be interested in the girl, but was actually planning to escape after mastering the magic techniques he was being taught. After a year, having become an expert sorcerer, he escaped from the clutches of the aborigines and returned to his parish.

'Those days, some of the powerful Namboodiri magicians were trying to prove that their powers were superior to that of the God worshipped by the Christians. This they did by challenging the Christian priests to magic duels, almost invariably defeating them and bringing dishonour to the Church. Kadamuttam changed all that. He defeated many well-known Namboodiri magicians with his powerful sorcery. Muttakad Srikandan Namboodiri's grandfather was one of them.

'Kadamuttam was best known for his power over Yakshis. It is said that...'

'Shut up, Sadasiva,' said Shunya, from behind.

'Sorry, Saami,' said Sadasivan and became silent. In a short while, they drove across the Karamana Bridge. They could hear the sound of the flowing water. In a few minutes, Sadasivan turned the car into a narrow mud track on the right side of the main road. After driving for two kilometres on the rough and dusty trail, they came to the foot of the hill. 'This is as far as we can drive,' said Sadasivan, 'I think we'll have to go on foot from here and then start climbing the hill.'

It was totally dark when the headlights were turned off. Sadasivan switched on the flashlight and they got out of the car. Thambi took out the shoulder bag which contained the few things that Shunya had asked him to take with him, and with Shunya leading the way, they started climbing. The climb was steep, and the roughly hewn path was rocky. At the end of a strenuous half an hour that literally bathed them in sweat, they reached what appeared to be the mouth of a cave. Sadasivan pulled out his sickle and chopped off the thorny bushes that covered it.

They found the entrance just big enough to crawl through. Shunya entered first, and Sadasivan and Thambi followed. They found themselves in a fairly large tunnel which had three smaller tunnels branching out from the right, and one from the left. Shunya chose the one on the left.

The rocky surface inside the tunnel was damp and had a musty odour. Walking carefully over the wet and slippery floor, they came to a heavy, crudely fashioned, oval wooden door with a rusted latch.

'If we had taken the right turn, we would have got lost in the labyrinth,' whispered Shunya, and using both his hands, managed to lift the latch with great effort.

The door creaked open. Sadasivan flashed the torch, and both he and Thambi screamed and jumped backwards. A gigantic black cobra, at least ten feet in length, with its hood expanded and hissing menacingly, stood guard, ready to strike anyone who dared to enter.

Shunya roared with laughter and said, 'You are bigger than your brown brother who tried to kill Meenakshi. Now move out of the way for your own good!'

While Sadasivan and Thambi looked on astonished, the snake lowered its head, turned, and slipped away into the darkness. 'Come, let's move,' Shunya said.

They now entered another tunnel which curved to the right and ended in a dimly lit, spacious cavern. As Sadasivan and Thambi followed Shunya into the cavern, they noticed that the light came from four ornate brass lamps that hung from the whitewashed ceiling, each with a wick that emitted a deep blue light. In the centre of the well-polished, black granite floor was a fairly large pit, in which blazed a sacrifical fire. On the right side of the pit was a human skull, and on the left, a copper brazier in which a special incense was being burnt. They realised that the musty odour which they had smelt even as they had entered the tunnel came from the incense. Now it was strong and overpowering. Sadasivan and Thambi felt their minds going hazy.

All of a sudden, a hidden door at the extreme end of the cavern opened and Siddhan made a dramatic entry shouting loudly, '*Hrrrh, hrrrh, hada hada, phat, phat.*' He was followed by the siren who had accompanied him when he had come visiting Shunya. She appeared even more sensous, wearing a transparent red nylon saree and gold anklets on her feet. Siddhan himself was naked except for a red kaupin which barely hid his private parts. His black skin glistened, and his face was painted grotesquely with white paint. In his right hand, he held a human thigh bone, and in his left hand was a small black-coloured drum.

'Ho, ho, ha, ha,' laughed Shunya, 'all this drama doesn't frighten me. Don't waste time. Do whatever you want to and get on with it.'

'We'll see, we'll see,' sneered Siddhan, 'so you have brought these two jokers with you. They'll die of sheer fear. Sit down here near the fire, in front of the skull, and I tell you, you'll regret the day you accepted my challenge. Crazy fool!'

'All that we shall see presently,' said Shunya, sitting cross-legged at the spot indicated. Sadasivan and Thambi, trembling with fear, sat down beside Shunya. 'Whatever happens,' said Shunya to them, 'do not panic and get up from here. Stay put, and I'll see that nothing happens to you. Where are the three limes, the pot of water, the candle and the matchbox I had asked you to carry?'

'Here, Saami,' said Thambi, and taking out the materials from the shoulder bag in which he had carried them, placed them on the floor, and untied the rubber sheet he had used to cover the mouth of the pot.

'Remember to give them to me when I ask for it,' said Shunya.

Siddhan sat on the other side of the fire pit, facing them, with the woman by his side. 'Oho! Tricks of the trade,' mocked Siddhan, looking at the pot and the lemons. Then he chanted, '*Ghum, bho, kata kata*, Bhairavi of the cremation grounds, *kreem, kreem*,' and threw a handful of incense from a wooden bowl into the fire. The fire flashed silver white for a split second, and the air was filled with a sweet, intoxicating scent.

Placing the bone and the drum on the floor by his side, Siddhan turned to his assistant and began to make what looked like hypnotic passes over her face. Speaking in a low voice, he said, 'Come on, Yakshini, come on you, who feeds on blood and eats corpses, manifest yourself with this fire as a witness, and destroy my enemies who sit before me. Come on, I command you, manifest yourself. *Kreem, hut, phat, hiri hiri.'*

An eerie moan came forth from the woman's lips and before Sadasivan and Thambi's terrified eyes, her face underwent a hideous transformation. It turned ugly and wrinkled. Her blood-shot eyes stared ferociously from their shrunken sockets and she opened her mouth wide, revealing sharp, fang-like canines and a blood-red tongue lolling out from between them, almost touching the chin.

She stood up, and with a jerk, threw away the nylon cloth that was draped around her body to reveal a tall, almost skeletal frame, jet black and shining. With a blood-curdling shriek, she turned in Shunya's direction and lunged at him.

'Give me the lime,' Shunya shouted, but Sadasivan and Thambi were rendered immobile with fear. They held each other's hands and just stared open-mouthed at the scene. Shunya was now standing up and making peculiar gestures with his outstretched arms. The fiend was trying hard but seemed physically unable to come too close to him. Shunya landed a hard kick on Thambi's back and screamed, 'Wake up, ass, and pass me the lime, quick!'

That broke the spell. Thambi sprang into action. Picking up a lime, he quickly handed it to Shunya. Sadasivan stood up, holding the water pot.

The ogress bolted forward, managed to clutch Shunya's

head with her clawed fingers, and tried to sink her fangs into his neck. Shunya pushed the lime into her open mouth, and using both his hands forced her to shut it. Then he knocked his forehead against hers with tremendous force. She swallowed the lime.

Within seconds, she let go of him. Shunya's shoulders were now bleeding from the deep cuts she had inflicted with her claws. 'Give me the knife,' shouted Shunya.

Sadasivan handed him the dagger. Yelling, 'Leave this body, Yakshi, go back to the burial ground, *phat, phat,*' Shunya drove the pointed end of the dagger into the crown of her head.

She wailed as if in great pain, vomited blood, closed her eyes and fell unconscious.

'Give me water,' said Shunya. Thambi brought the pot to him. Shunya sprinkled the water on her now prostrate body, from the head to the toes. In seconds, she was transformed back to her original, beautiful form. Opening her eyes, she looked around, and then at her own body. Realising that she was naked, she ran out of the cavern without a word.

Siddhan, who had till then been shocked into silence, found his voice and shouted after her, 'Wait, Seema, don't run away. We'll teach this fellow a lesson he'll never forget.' But it was of no use. She never came back.

'So what's your new trick, you son of a she-devil?' taunted Shunya.

'You think you have won?' roared Siddhan, his eyes redder than ever. Still squating in front of the fire, he put a bottle of strong arrack to his lips, and emptied it at one go. Then he belched noisily and said, 'You have seen nothing yet. I shall now invoke the king of all evil, Kutti-chathan, who will destroy you forever.'

'Go ahead,' said Shunya, and sat down again. 'You two,' he said, turning to Sadasivan and Thambi, 'sit down in the same place.' He then reached out and drew an imaginary circle around them. 'Under no circumstances should you move out of this circle,' he said.

Siddhan threw more incense into the brazier, and the odour of the whitish smoke became almost unbearable. Then he opened a cane basket which was on his right side. Pulling a struggling black cock out of it, he held it over the fire and cut its throat. As the blood of the bird fell on the fire, a horrible cackle was heard coming from inside the pit. Having drained the blood, Siddhan threw away the bird and stared intensly at the fire. He started to beat the little drum and chanted at the top of his voice, 'Kutti-chatha, Lord of all evil-doers, chief of the devils, come, come; I invoke you to manifest yourself here and now. Leave your abode of lovely, stinking corpses, and come here immediately. *Hroom, hreem, hura, hura, koodhichoodha, kunnanatha, pannupannu, humphat.*'

A nauseating smell of decaying corpses filled the air. Suddenly, a large ball of fire appeared before their eyes and exploded to reveal a small, obese, brown-complexioned figure, just about two feet in height, with a face so ugly and frightful that Sadsivan and Thambi began to tremble.

Its face was a cross between a gorilla and a human. The eyes were almost human but the rest of the face was that of a hairy ape, with razor-sharp canines, bared and ready to attack. The body was entirely hairless and glistening, except for a long, furry tail.

'Aha, aha, Kutti-chatha, attack this man,' shouted Siddhan, grinning widely and pointing at Shunya, 'he is your food today. Drink the blood of this enemy of ours. Destroy him forever.'

The creature fixed its eyes on Shunya, growled, swished its tail, and flashing its murderous fangs, went straight for Shunya's throat. Shunya, who seemed to have been taken by surprise, was thrown to the floor with the creature clinging on to him with his arms and legs, and attempting to bury its fangs into his neck. Blood flowed from Shunya's neck as his carotid was punctured. They rolled on the ground locked in combat, while Siddhan kept shouting, 'Kill him! Drink his blood! Kill him!'

'Light the candle,' yelled Shunya, 'quick!'

With trembling hands, Sadasivan and Thambi lit the candle, and together went towards the combatants. The creature, seeing the candle, let go of Shunya, and howling like a wolf, sprang towards them.

Shunya snatched the candle from Thambi, and shouted, 'Go back to your place! Don't move from there!' They ran back into the protective circle, just in time. The creature moved around the circle, growling and making threatening gestures, unable to get in. It then turned back to Shunya.

Shunya held the lighted candle in his right hand and traced an imaginary pentacle in the air with the flame. With that, the ghoul found itself unable to move closer. It stood facing Shunya, and let out an angry howl. Shunya chanted, *'Humphat, koodi koodi, madamada, phat phat,'* and picking up the dagger, plunged it into its chest. The creature whined and fell backwards. A viscous yellow fluid oozed out of the wound. Pointing to Siddhan, Shunya shouted, 'Catch him before he runs away, Kutti-chatha, he is responsible for luring you into this trap! Don't let him escape!'

The creature pulled the dagger out of its chest and threw it into the fire. Then, with a fierce growl, it leapt on Siddhan. Felling him to the ground, it punctured his jugular vein with its fangs and began to drink his blood. 'No!' screamed Siddhan, struggling to free himself from its grip, but it was of no use. Within minutes, he was unconscious.

The creature, satiated with the bloody nourishment, turned itself into a ball of fire, and disappeared into the fire-pit. Shunya threw the remaining water, the candle and the limes into the fire, and turning to Sadasivan and Thambi said, 'Let's get out of here now. This fellow Siddhan isn't dead. He will recover after a while, but he will trouble us no more. Come on, you two, let's go.'

With Shunya flashing Sadasivan's torch and leading the way, they hurried through the maze of tunnels and managed to get out. Dawn was just breaking when they started walking down the hill.

Sadasivan was relieved to find the car standing exactly where he had parked it. They climbed in and sat in total silence till the car crossed the bridge across the Karamana River. Then Sadasivan sighed deeply and said, 'Saami, honestly, I thought I was going to die.'

'I did, too,' said Thambi. 'What was all that, Saami?'

'Nothing,' said Shunya, 'nothing at all. There was no Yakshi, no kutti-chathan, no nothing. It was all an illusion. You two were hallucinating because you had breathed in copious quantities of the smoke produced by burning hemp, dried shells of crabs, and dried bull-shit, all mixed together. Actually, there were only three of you: you two, and Siddhan. Shunya is nothing and cannot be counted. Ha! Ha! What a phantasmagoria! Just like the rest of the world. Nothing from nothing, something from nothing, but Shunyam saw nothing, heard nothing, said nothing. No-thing!'

'But, Saami, you were yourself badly injured...'

Seeing Thambi's gaze upon him, Shunya said sternly, 'Shut up.' And that was the end of the discussion.

ॐ

Sadasivan dropped Shunya and Thambi at the toddy shop and went home. 'Let's go for our morning walk,' said Shunya to Thambi, 'and then we'll have a bath in the temple pond. Are you tired?'

'No,' said Thambi, 'I don't feel tired at all. It's all your magic, Saami, I am ready.'

That morning while they walked, Shunya talked to Thambi a great deal about reality and illusion.

31

Ten days after the Karamana Hill episode, a top secret, closed-door meeting, attended by a handful of carefully selected people, took place in the private home-office of the minister late in the evening.

Apart from the minister himself, the monk who was his Guru, a high-ranking member of the Church, a prominent Mosque Committee functionary and a toddy shop owner who was jealous of Sadasivan's good fortune, were among those who were present.

The consensus arrived at after a great deal of discussion was that Shunya had to go. He was too dangerous to society. All norms were being thrown to the winds, all religions were being criticised and ridiculed, religious practices were being made fun of, the very fundamentals of organised religion were being questioned, and many more Westerners were coming in. It was time to end the drama before he became more popular and powerful.

And if he were really a lunatic, which some were convinced he was, then all the more reason to get rid of him. No one could, however, come to a conclusion as to how he was to be eliminated. After an hour of serious deliberation, they parted on the note that the minister, being a senior politician, would perhaps find a way.

'All right,' said the veteran politician finally, 'leave it to me. Let me work on this. I think I know who can do the job.'

'Just make sure it doesn't turn out to be like the amateurish attempt they made to burn him alive, inside his cottage. The fellow actually became more famous after that fiasco,' said his Guru.

'This is going to be foolproof,' said the minister.

The next morning, Shekharan, a special representative of the politician, contacted Khader, a notorious hitman, who, with his powerful connections, had escaped being prosecuted for half-a-dozen homicide charges.

Khader, retired from what was referred to as 'active business', was then living in Quilon, a small coastal town sixty kilometres from Thiruvananthapuram. He owned a fishing trawler and was looked upon as a hero, a sort of a leader in the community of fishermen among whom he lived. Judging by their standards, he was wealthy and lived in a reasonably good house not far from the seashore with his wife and grown-up son, who assisted him in the fishing business.

Shekharan met him in his house and explained the reason for his visit.

'Look here, Shekhar-anna,' said Khader, 'first of all, big boss knows that I have retired from active business for the last six years. To start again now would not be easy, and, I think, also unwise.'

'I understand,' said Shekharan, 'but the boss says you have suffered some bad losses and you need money for your son's wedding...'

'Let's go for a walk,' said Khader, and they walked out of the house to the beach.

The sea was blue-green and since it was high tide, extremely turbulent. Huge waves broke on the shore, spraying water on their faces even at a distance.

'They are all my boats,' said Khader, pointing towards half-a-dozen traditional fishing boats that were stationed on the sands, 'the sea is very rough. Only a few boats will go in today.'

The sun was hot but the cool, fresh sea-breeze was pleasant. Little boys played on the sands, some flying kites, some wading in the water, little naked bodies playing games with the formidable sea.

'My trawler has been sent for repairs,' said Khader, 'costs a lot of money.'

'The boss is willing to offer you twenty-five thousand rupees.'

Khader spat loudly into the sand. 'He thinks I am so cheap, what?'

'No, no,' said Shekharan, getting a little nervous. It suddenly occurred to him that he was alone, standing near the sea, with a brutal, cold-blooded murderer. 'Boss asked me to negotiate with you.'

Khader smiled, folded up his bright blue lungi, and tying a knot, fastened it to the waist securely. He said, 'He is a clever man. Now tell me about this bird who is to be sacrificed.'

Shekharan gave him a fairly descriptive account, not forgetting to add that he lived in a toddy shop and insulted Islam by ridiculing circumcision.

Khader listened carefully, stroking his beard and scratching his bald pate. Shekharan noticed the bulging muscles rippling under Khader's tight t-shirt. At last, Khader said, 'Shouldn't be difficult to finish off this fellow but fifty thousand is the rate. Not one rupee less. Tell the boss and get back to me. I have to go for my Friday prayers now. I must get to know by today evening. You can go now.'

Shekharan left immediately. He was back by evening. 'Here,' he said, 'is half the money, twenty-five thousand. The rest you get after the deed. Is that okay?'

'Fair enough,' said Khader, 'tell the boss that I require a day or two to execute the deed. He doesn't have to worry about it now.'

For the next two days, Khader did his own reconnaissance. From a safe distance, he studied Shunya's movements, and those of his followers. By Sunday, he had worked out a plan. The best time would be when Shunya went out for his customary walk in the morning in the coconut grove. He had the strategy worked out to precision. He would hide in the bushes behind the temple pond and take aim.

On Sunday evening, he took out his Webley & Scott revolver which he hadn't touched in a long time, cleaned, checked, and loaded it.

On Monday morning, at six-thirty, as Shunya walked past the bushes with Thambi in tow, Khader took aim and fired. Khader had always prided himself on the fact that he had never had to fire more than one shot to hit the bullseye. He had aimed at the heart and pulled the trigger.

Shunya gave a loud cry and fell down. Thambi screamed, 'Saami, Saami,' and fell on him, trying to protect him.

With absolute certainty that the job was done, Khader slipped away quietly from behind the bushes, ran up the adjoining hillock and came down on the other side. From there, he had only to get on to the main road by crossing a shallow nullah. Just as he stepped on the road, he saw a police jeep passing by.

Khader climbed onto his motorbike which he had parked under a tamarind tree, and coolly rode back to Quilon.

Meanwhile, hearing the sound of the gunfire and Thambi's scream that followed, some of the volunteers ran to the coconut grove. They were followed by the devotees who had stayed the night at the 'kull ashram'. Someone ran to Sadasivan's house to inform him. The police inspector who was passing by heard the commotion and rushed in with two or three policemen.

Seeing that Shunya was motionless and that blood was flowing down his shoulder and chest on the left side, Thambi and some of the others started crying. Sadasivan and Bhavani arrived. Seeing the situation, Bhavani started beating her breast and wailing, 'Ayyo, Saami! Have you gone, leaving us orphans?' Sadasivan held Bhavani's hands trying to restrain her and started crying himself.

'Let me see,' said the inspector, pushing everybody aside, 'will you let me do my job?' He kneeled down beside Shunya, felt his pulse and said, 'The pulse is beating.'

'Why won't it beat?' said the familiar voice of Shunya. The inspector was startled. 'Thank God,' he said, 'greetings, Saami!' After the incident when he had raided Shunya's cottage on the minister's instructions, Chandu Nair was convinced that Shunya possessed magical powers. He certainly was not an ordinary man. He had come to believe that with Shunya anything was possible.

'Thambi, stop howling and give me a hand,' said Shunya. 'And you, Sadasiva, Bhavani, has anybody died that you are making such a racket? Stop it!'

Assisted by Thambi, Shunya slowly walked back to the courtyard. His white loincloth was drenched in blood.

'Let's take him to the hospital,' said the inspector.

'Nothing doing,' said Shunya, 'nobody is taking Shunya anywhere. Bring me some black tea.'

A German visitor, Dr Hans, came forward and said, 'Saami, can I look at the wound? I am a doctor.'

'Okay,' said Shunya.

Dr Hans asked for some clean cloth. There was no spirit available so the doctor had to make use of a bottle of brandy that someone produced. He cleaned the blood that had flowed down the chest and shoulders.

'Nothing serious,' said the doctor, 'but it could have been lethal. Gunshot from a small revolver and the bullet just grazed his left shoulder. Luckily, it didn't enter the bone.'

He quickly cleaned the wound and tied a temporary bandage around it. Soon, Dr Bhaskar Menon, who someone had gone to fetch, came with a nurse. He had a few words with Dr Hans, checked the wound, and then instructed the nurse to do a proper dressing.

Shunya kept repeating in English, 'Thank you, thank you, thank you.'

Dr Menon said, 'Saami, it is a good idea to take an injection, a tetanus toxoid.'

'No injections,' said Shunya.

'Can anybody tell me what happened?' asked the inspector.

Everybody seemed to speak at once and the inspector shouted, 'Silence, please! Can any one person speak? Thambi?'

'I'll tell you,' said Shunya. 'Now will the rest of you including the doctors go and mind your own business? Only Thambi, Sada, Bhavani and the inspector may stay here.'

'Now,' said Shunya to the inspector, 'somebody took a shot, with the intention of killing Shunya. You see that? To kill Shunya. The bullet grazed Shunya's shoulder. Go look in the coconut grove, you'll find it. Sadasiva, bring me my tea.'

'I have it ready,' said Sadasivan.

'Okay, then give it to me, and all of you go. Shunya is fine, as empty as ever.'

'You need to write a report, Saami,' said the inspector. 'File an F.I.R., a First Information Report.'

'Shunya will file no report, no F.I.R.,' said Shunya, and entering the cottage, shut the door and bolted it from inside.

'You have to file an F.I.R.,' said the inspector to Sadasivan as they went out together. Like a watchdog, Thambi sat in the courtyard in front of the cottage.

'I think Shunya needs protection,' said Sadasivan to the police inspector. The inspector shook his head, and went back with his constables to the coconut grove to look for evidence, wondering if the minister was involved. If he was, he knew there would be no point in investigating further. The minister was too powerful.

A .22 bullet was discovered. An F.I.R. was filed at the police station by Sadasivan.

32

As Khader rode back to his house, he noticed something peculiar, something that had never happened to him before. The face of the man he had been hired to kill kept appearing before his mind's eye. It remained with him when he had his lunch, and even during his evening prayers.

In the evening, he went to the telephone booth at the post office, rang up the minister directly and said, 'Boss, I have done my job. When do I get the rest of the money?'

The boss was livid with rage. He retorted, 'What job? The man is alive with a minor wound. He will become more of a hero now, you stupid fisherman! And how dare you call me on the telephone? What if somebody overhears? Anyway, I am not asking you to return the advance...'

At this point, anger rose like a red-hot flame and burst forth through Khader's vocal cords. 'You fucking bastard,' he said between clenched teeth, and cut off the connection.

At dinner, he was in a very irritable mood. 'Too much salt in the khurma,' he grumbled, 'one of these days I'll be dead from an overdose of salt. Good medicine for high B.P.'

At night as he lay in bed, still thinking of the strange man he had somehow missed killing at such close quarters, Khatija, his wife, came and stood beside him.

'What's the matter?' he asked.

'You won't get angry with me if I ask you something?'

'Angry with you? No, no, Khati, you are the rose of my heart, my darling wife, my...' He pulled her hand, and made her sit on the bed.

'Shhh! Don't make so much noise,' she said, 'Babu is sleeping in the next room.'

'Okay, okay, and what did my queen want to say?'

'Tell me, didn't you promise me you'll never again go back to that bad business? Why did you do it again? You think I don't know? You loaded the gun and took it out today. There is one bullet missing.

Why go back to evil again? Why?' She began to cry.

Khader sat up, and tried to console her, 'Khati, your prayers seem to have saved me. That man escaped with a minor wound. I was only trying to get some money. The trawler is...'

'Take all my jewellery and sell it,' she said, still crying, 'only, don't go back to a life of crime please. Throw that gun in the sea, I beg you.'

'There, there,' said Khader, 'I promise, never again. I'll throw the gun away. They told me, this man is an infidel who ridicules Islam and so on. What is the harm in killing an infidel, I thought. You know...'

'Doesn't Allah know how to deal with infidels?' said Khatija, 'that excuse is just rubbish. Only Allah can decide whose life is to be taken and whose to be given. You are nobody to do that. All these maulvis, they think they are God's agents. Allah needs no agents. We have no right to take anybody's life.'

'Anyway, something peculiar is going on,' said Khader, 'that man I was hired to kill, his face keeps haunting me. Some say he is a lunatic and some call him Shunya Saami. He lives in a toddy shop.'

'I have also heard of him,' said Khatija, 'maybe he is a holy man, a Mastan, a God-intoxicated one, or a Wali, a friend of God, a saint.'

'Can't be,' said Khader, 'he lives in a toddy shop and doesn't pray five times a day.'

'So? Allah has his mysterious ways. How can mortals like you and me comprehend his ways? Mastans tend to behave strangely sometimes. The best thing for you would be to go and seek his blessings. Don't tell him anything that will link you with the deed. Just sit before him, pray silently and come away. I'll come with you if you want.'

'No, I'll go alone,' said Khader, 'but first, I'll go and throw that gun into the sea.'

'You are my precious pearl,' said Khatija, and kissed him on his cheek.

'I'll be back soon. Don't sleep before I come, we have important work to do,' said Khader before leaving.

'Chi! Always saying dirty things,' said Khatija, and giggled.

33

The very next morning, Khader went to Thiruvananthapuram. At eleven, a muscular man, well past middle-age, who walked like an ex-wrestler, approached Sadasivan.

'My name is Khader,' he said. 'Is it possible to meet Saami?'

'You can meet him in the evening at six during general satsang,' said Sadasivan, 'Normally, he…'

Just then Thambi arrived. 'Saami asked you to send in the stranger who has come looking for him right away,' he said.

'Here, this is the person who has come,' said Sadasivan.

Thambi lead Khader to Shunya, who was waiting under the jackfruit tree.

'Come,' he said, 'and sit down. Shunya has been waiting for you. Thambi, this time I don't want you to take notes or be present.'

Thambi walked away.

'Now,' said Shunya, 'what is the matter?'

'First, sir, I came to apologise and seek forgiveness, and I am going to be frank. My name is Khader and I was the one who was hired to kill you. Actually, my wife Khatija feels you are a holy man, although she hasn't seen you. She persuaded me to seek your forgiveness. She also told me not to speak a word but to silently sit before you and pray for forgiveness but I couldn't control myself when I saw you and now I have told you the truth.

'This was the first killing I attempted after many years,

and I have promised to myself and to my wife that I will stop from now on. I have thrown my gun into the sea. Thank God you escaped, and I don't know how you did, because I am a sharpshooter and I never miss.'

'Does not matter,' said Shunya, patting him on his back, 'look forward and forget the past. You say your wife said that Shunya is a holy man. What do you think?'

'I don't know,' said Khader, 'but you seem to have a strange effect on me. Somehow I am beginning to feel that my stone heart is melting. Really, sir...'

'Don't say sir, call me Appa.'

'Really, Appa, I had given up the life of a criminal a long time ago, but then I was badly in need of money. They said you criticised our religion and were an infidel, and I thought...but you are so kind. If you say so, I can go to the police and make a clean breast of the affair. That fellow, the minister, deserves nothing better. They may arrest me for attempted murder but I know how to come out of prison soon.'

'No,' said Shunya, 'don't tell anyone. Just keep quiet and don't repeat such actions. Listen to these stories about the founder of your religion.

'It is said that he once found a deadly scorpion drowning in a small water tank. He thrust his hand inside and tried to lift it out of the water. The scorpion stung. He let go and tried again. It stung again. He is said to have tried seven times, got stung seven times and finally got the scorpion out of the water.

'That is the kindness and compassion that should come out of religion. Animals kill for food, out of hunger. And what do you kill for? Money...'

'But the Prophet went to war against unbelievers,' said Khader.

'Are you a Prophet? Did you get an order from your God to kill? Lots of people in lunatic asylums are there because they believe they were ordered by God to kill somebody.

'Be that as it may, don't go back to your old ways now. Here, look into my eyes. Why would you kill a harmless nothing with no mind? The mind has gone to pieces; there is only peace of mind.'

Khader looked into Shunya's eyes. Remorse swept through his psyche. A profound sadness gripped his being, and for the first time in many years Khader wept. His whole body shook as he cried.

Shunya stroke his head and shoulders saying, 'Shunya, Shunya, nothingness, let go.'

Khader wiped his tears, and held Shunya's feet with both hands, saying, 'Bless me, Appa, my father.'

'Be at peace,' said Shunya, placing both his hands on Khader's head. Khader returned to Quilon.

'Khatija,' he said to his wife, 'I start a new life from now. Appa is a...is a...I really don't know; something great. We should go and see him together at least once.'

They visited him many times. Shunya told them many stories of the Sufi saints. Khatija's and Khader's favourite story was that of the ancient Sufi saint, Mansoor al-Hallaj. Shunya would himself be in ecstasy while relating the stories and the couple would shed tears profusely.

'Mansoor al-Hallaj,' Shunya said, 'after going on pilgrimages to many holy places, eventually settled down at Baghdad. Once he was overwhelmed by the ecstasy of the union with the Supreme Void, whom he called his beloved. So absorbed was he in the unity of his experience that only 'the beloved' remained and Mansoor's personal identity was totally destroyed.

'He therefore proclaimed in public, "I am the Truth."
This was blasphemy according to Muslim law. Recognising
his great spiritual stature, the Caliph requested him to
retract and seek pardon. He was in no mood to do so
and declared that he was speaking the truth.

'The Caliph, supported by the theologians, then put
him through horrendous torture. His limbs were amputated
and his eyes gouged. With a smile, he continued to say
"I am the Truth." Finally, his tongue was cut off so that
he may never again utter the words and equate himself
with the Almighty Lord. His body was then burnt and
the ashes thrown into the sea.

'They say the ocean reverberated with the sound of
"I am the Truth."'

One day, Shunya asked them what it was that they
desired most in life. 'Two things,' they said together, 'one
is that you remain always in our heart and the other is to
visit the holy shrine of Mecca before we die.'

'Both shall be fulfilled,' said Shunya. 'Shunya shall always
be in your hearts and as for Mecca, why not right now?
Khader, bring me my water pot, it is inside my cottage.'

Khader entered the cottage for the first time. To him,
it was like entering the abode of the sacred. In one corner,
he located the clay water pot and carried it out carefully,
wondering what Shunya had meant when he said 'as for
Mecca, why not right now?'

Shunya threw the water away, emptied it and hit the
bottom of the pot with his right palm, making a sound
similar to the sound of the ghattam, a special clay pot
used by south Indian percussionists.

'Now, you two,' he said, 'keep your faces close to the
mouth of the pot and look inside.'

At first, they saw nothing but darkness. Then a misty white screen appeared. The screen parted and they beheld before their startled eyes hundreds of people in white, circumambulating the Kaaba. They saw themselves joining the pilgrims in the circumambulation.

Overpowered by emotion, Khatija wept and fainted. Khader sat in silence, his body trembling with emotion.

Just then, Thambi appeared. 'Thambi, take the pot, fill it with water and put it back in the cottage,' said Shunya.

'Yes, Saami,' said Thambi and took away the water pot.

That day, when Khatija and Khader were starting to go back home, Shunya said to them, 'Khader, you and your wife need not come here anymore. What you see here is a mere shadow whose essence is the Infinite Void, Shunya. Both of you practise what I have taught you, and find Shunya within your hearts.'

'Whatever you say, hazrath,' they said and departed with tears in their eyes.

Khader became a rich man with several fishing trawlers. He abandoned his old ways. Till the end, they obeyed Shunya's command and didn't go to visit him. Eventually, when they died, everyone marvelled at the extraordinary way they passed away.

One evening, three years after Shunya had disappeared as mysteriously as he had appeared, Khader and Khatija sat side by side on their prayer mats, as they did every day while praying, finished their prayers, and never got up.

The neighbours found them the next morning, lying dead beside each other on their prayer mats with a smile on their lips. Arifa, the first neighbour to enter the house, said that she heard music, as if someone was playing the flute, when she entered the house, but no one paid much attention to her.

The local Muslims built a tomb for them on the seashore, and it came to be known as the mausoleum of Saint Khader and Saint Khatija. People of all communities came to pray, prostrate, and seek the blessings of the departed saints.

34

Ten days after Khader's conversion, Shunya did something extraordinary even by his own eccentric and unpredictable standards.

It was 6 p.m. on a Friday, and a crowd had gathered for the general satsang. Someone in the crowd asked, 'Can you defy death? Has anybody come back after dying?'

'Nobody,' said Shunya, 'have you seen the letters R.I.P. on the tombstones in Christian graveyards? They say that it means 'Rest in Peace', but I think it is 'Rise if Possible'. A challenge. No one can do it.'

'But they say that yogis can do it.'

'Oh that, well, Shunya will show you something.'

Then, shouting loudly, 'Here I go, wait for six hours,' Shunya stretched out full length under the jackfruit tree, and lay like a dead body.

After a brief, shocked silence, there was general pandemonium. Everybody rushed towards Shunya as he lay prostrate. A cacophony of voices erupted.

'Call the doctor!'

'No, take him to the hospital!'

'First see what has happened, maybe he is sleeping.'

'What do you mean, sleeping?'

'He is actually in a trance, Samadhi.'

'Someone called Har Har Baba was given up for dead for three days, and then he came back.'

'Impossible!'

Sadasivan and Thambi, with the help of the other devotees, managed to bring some order. With great difficulty, they persuaded the crowd to move. Meanwhile, some were seen prostrating before the still body and trying to touch his feet. The inspector came with his constables and sent everybody away. Only Thambi, Sadasivan, the inspector and Dr Hans remained.

Dr Bhaskar Menon arrived after a few minutes, followed by Bhavani who was crying and lamenting loudly, 'Ayyo, Saami! Why did you do this? Why do you play such terrible games? I can't bear to live without you. Aiyoo!'

Sadasivan wiped his own tears and took charge. 'Bhavani, stop crying,' he said, 'if you have faith in Saami, then you mustn't cry. Saami said, "Wait for six hours." I am sure he'll come back. Don't you remember how he didn't die even after he was shot?'

Bhavani managed to control her grief, and sitting near Shunya's feet, started to meditate and pray with closed eyes. Thambi was absolutely calm. He told Dr Hans and Dr Menon, 'Doctors, please examine him.'

Dr Hans checked Shunya's pulse, heartbeat and breathing, and shook his head slowly. He whispered to Thambi, 'No sign of life. No pulse, no breathing.'

Dr Menon also arrived at the same conclusion. 'But, what do we do now?' he asked.

The inspector took the doctors aside, 'What do you think?' he asked them.

'Clinically, he is dead,' said Dr Menon. 'I agree,' said Dr Hans, 'but since he has asked everyone to wait for six hours, I think it would be wise to do so.'

Dr Menon pursed his lips and ran his fingers through his hair. 'Actually I think Dr Hans is right. We should wait and not do anything in haste. Yogis sometimes perform puzzling feats, though I must admit that this is the first time I am dealing with one. Some say he is an Avadhuta, a sage who is free of all social norms. He may be a madman, as some others think, but why not wait? Why not give him the benefit of the doubt?'

Dr Hans said, 'I have read that a fakir, Haridas, once went into a trance and was buried under the earth for forty days in 1837 in Maharaja Ranjit Singh's court at Lahore. According to a book published in 1850 called *Observations on Trance or, Human Hibernation*, by James Braid, the physician who had coined the term 'hypnosis', the fakir came back to life at the end of it.

'He based his report on a perfectly authenticated paper written by Sir Claude Wade, the British resident at the Maharaja's court, who was present on the occasion. It looks like some kind of a voluntary hibernation technique. For instance, certain animals naturally hibernate in winter, but I must say that this is the first time I have seen something like this. I also think that we should wait.'

The inspector, who hadn't forgotten the incident of his son's birthday sweets, and having seen the remarkable way Shunya conducted himself when he was shot, tended to think that there was more to Shunya than met the eye. He relented.

'Okay,' he said, 'if the doctors say so. Normally, I would have insisted on a medical report and then made arrangements for the post-mortem, but we'll wait.'

Bhavani was still praying with closed eyes. Someone had lit a small brass oil-lamp and the smell of frankincense rose from the clay incense burner.

Thambi had covered the body with a white cloth, leaving the face uncovered. After consulting him, Sadasivan let the devotees sit at a safe distance from the body in the courtyard. They were requested to remain silent.

Someone wanted to sing devotional songs, but Thambi and Sadasivan were against it. 'Let's maintain silence,' they insisted.

The news spread quickly. Many people arrived at the scene. Some remained to see what would happen, others went away. Some said it was futile to wait because he was dead. Others thought that he would revive. Newspaper reporters and photographers went about their work. The faithful kept vigil.

Bhavani, tired, leaned against the jackfruit tree and fell asleep. Thambi and Sadasivan remained awake. Some volunteers monitored the visitors.

Dr Hans sat beside the body. Every now and then, he would examine it. Dr Menon had returned home. The inspector left, promising to be back later. Extra lights had been installed to light up the courtyard.

Around midnight, Bhavani woke up. She sat down near Shunya's head, stroking his forehead softly, while tears trickled down her cheeks.

At five minutes to twelve, the inspector returned, accompanied by the politician. At twelve sharp, the politician said to the inspector, 'What are you waiting for now? You think the dead man will come alive? Take the body and do the post-mortem.'

Thambi pleaded, 'Please let us wait for a few more minutes.'

Bhavani lifted Shunya's feet and placed them on her bosom. 'I won't let go,' she said between sobs.

'Do your duty,' the politician said to the inspector.

M.K. strode in from the street. 'Nobody should do anything,' he said gravely, 'perhaps he is dead, but it is better to wait for a while.'

'Oh! M.K., the great Marxist, is also a devotee of Shunya,' said the politician derisively, 'how wonderful!'

'You stay out of this,' said M.K. to the politician.

'Why should I?' asked the politician, his voice raised.

'Because Shunya is alive, you son of a sow,' said Shunya, sitting up. 'Hey! What is all this weeping going on for, Bhavani? Who died?'

Everyone turned towards him in amazement. Cameras flashed.

'He is alive, he is alive!' everyone seemed to shout together.

'He never died!' shouted Shunya, standing up. He moved towards M.K. and, with his right hand, stroked the crown of M.K.'s head gently. M.K.'s eyes filled with tears. 'Saami,' was all that he uttered in a broken voice, before turning around and walking away.

The inspector fell at his feet and with folded hands said, 'Saami, forgive me. You are God!'

'Don't be funny,' said Shunya, 'this is nothing. Khechari Mudra, hatha yogic feat with tongue turned up and shutting the epiglottis. Shunya is nothing. Enjoy yourself. Sadasiva, Bhavani, children, go home. Shunya is not dead, Shunya loves you. You, Thambi, come with me.'

With that, Shunya strode into the cottage with Thambi in tow and shut the door.

Sadasivan announced, 'Please, everybody, go home now. General satsang is on Tuesday.'

Slowly, the crowd dispersed. The politician, planning his next move, went home in his posh car.

The inspector started his motorbike and went home in a daze. After his customary peg or two of rum and coke, he said to his wife, 'That Shunya is a real holy man. Now I am fully convinced. He came back from the dead.'

Sadasivan and Bhavani drove home in their Fiat Elegant.

'I have no doubt that he is Krishna, my God,' said Bhavani.

'He rose from the dead,' said Sadasivan. 'Only God can do that. He is so self-effacing that he wants to deny it. That story about the hatha yogic technique is meant to deliberately mislead. And the dog Ponnu didn't turn up this evening. I feel it's a bad omen.'

∾

Once inside the cottage, Shunya said, 'Thambi, you must be tired. Go to sleep.'

As Thambi unrolled his sleeping-mat, wondering if his own excited nerves could be put to sleep, Shunya spoke, 'Did you notice? Ponnu didn't turn up for the night.

'Ponnu is gone. We travelled together. Shunya came back while Ponnu didn't. Tell Sada he won't come back ever and no more questions about Ponnu from him or from you. Is that clear?'

'Yes, Saami.'

'Now sleep.'

As Thambi tried to sleep, he heard Shunya weeping piteously in the dark. Never before had Thambi seen or heard Shunya crying.

As sleep stole in slowly and softly, the sounds became muffled and finally vanished. The silence of sleep took over.

The next morning, when Sadasivan met Thambi, Thambi told him what Shunya had said about Ponnu. Sadasivan, in turn, related his experiences with Ponnu. The story was entered in Thambi's notebook.

35

Both the English and the local language dailies carried the story. Journalists arrived from far and near, seeking interviews, but Shunya refused to discuss what had happened.

The Saami Seva Sangham (S.S.S.), a small group of volunteers organised by Sadasivan to look after Shunya's needs and protect him from the curiosity seekers, was finding it more and more difficult to manage the mammoth crowds that began to gather from all over. More volunteers were recruited, and functionaries were designated to perform specific duties. Sadasivan became the president of the organisation.

As the crowds grew, Shunya became less and less accessible. He stopped going out for walks and spent more time inside the cottage. Sadasivan installed an attached bathroom and toilet for him, because it was impossible to go to the pond for a bath without the fear of being mobbed. The evening satsangs were reduced to one day in a week, and the personal interviews were stopped altogether, except when Shunya specially asked for someone.

Only Sadasivan, Thambi and Bhavani had free access to him.

At one such weekly satsang, Pappanaban, the local barber, came fully drunk. Shunya flew into a rage. 'Stop drinking, you fool,' he screamed, 'some bastards are drinking toddy and arrack and brandy, and pretending to be liberated and enlightened because Shunya lives in a toddy shop.

'Ramakrishna Paramahansa said to his followers, "If

I stand up and pee, you guys will pee going round in circles."

'If Shunyam stays in a toddy shop, you guys will drink a dozen bottles of brandy and pretend to be enlightened. Now bring me some toddy,' shouted Shunya.

In no time, Sadasivan produced a bottle. Shunya turned the bottle upside down, and emptied it under the jackfruit tree. He then tossed the bottle away with a flourish. The bottle landed in front of Pappanaban. He considered it a special blessing and took the bottle home. He installed it in a special place, and bowed down to it regularly, and lit incense before it for many years until his death. He called it 'Saami Kuppi, Saami's bottle'.

Many years after Pappanaban's death, the bottle was buried with religious ceremonies, and a little tomb-like structure was built upon it. Black tea was the prescribed offering at the tomb, and many swore that great miracles took place if one offered black tea there and prayed sincerely. It came to be known as 'Kuppi Samadhi, the tomb of the bottle'.

On that day, after the ceremony of the tossed toddy bottle, Shunya called the satsang to a close by announcing, 'Now the kathakali is over. Everybody can go home. The actor is retiring. Switch off the cameras, switch off the floodlights, nothing goes back to nothing. *Shunyam Eva Jayate*, Victory to the Void.'

Then he stood up and went into the cottage, taking Thambi with him.

36

Inside the cottage, Shunya sat cross-legged on his old mat and beckoned Thambi to come close to him. 'Sit here,' he said, 'Shunya is going soon. Has to go. Time is up.'

Shunya's words hit Thambi like a bombshell. He was struck dumb.

'Don't stare like an idiot,' Shunya said. 'Go and ask Sada to come here, now.'

Thambi sprang up and ran to get Sadasivan. In a few minutes, both Thambi and Sadasivan were sitting before Shunya.

'The Void is going back to the Void,' said Shunya. 'Break up the Sangam. Shunya wants no organisation. Break up the Sangam as soon as Shunya is gone. Shunya has no successors, no known disciples, no religion. You stay good friends. Let those who wish to know more read Thambi's notes. Thambi shall be guided by Shunya, but Thambi has work to do, understand?'

'Yes, Saami, all that I think I understand, but please don't go. Where will you go leaving us? Don't leave us please,' pleaded Sadasivan, prostrating at Shunya's feet.

'No-thing comes from nowhere, and goes nowhere,' said Shunya, 'no one can stop it. Disband the organisation. Bhavani is destined to bear a child. Thambi will marry Diana. Inform Bob after Shunya goes into nothingness.

'Shunya shall leave something behind. Keep it safe. When Kabir Das, the weaver saint, died, Hindus and Muslims fought for his body, claiming him as theirs. The cloth that covered the body was lifted and only a handful of flowers were found.

'Shunya will also leave something valuable, the essence. Keep it safe. Don't inform Bhavani about Shunya's wish to disappear. She will come to know herself.

'Now Sadasiva, you go home. Thambi, you stay.'

After Sadasivan's departure, Shunya said to Thambi, 'You begin your work right now.

'Go to Poojappura and meet Shunya's dear friend, Father Joseph. You'll find him in a tiny isolated cottage in a coconut grove, two furlongs from the Poojappura junction. Just take a right turn opposite the Shiva temple.

'We are linked to each other, though he never came to see Shunya. When you meet him, treat him with great humility. Convey my greetings and tell him that Shunya is going back to the Void soon.

'Then say the following: Shunya said to tell you that at your stage of evolution, the study of the Torah and the Talmud are completed. Give more attention to the Zohar of Rabbi Simeon bar Yochai.

'Since, like the great sage Jesus said, your eye is now single, between the eyebrows, your whole body is full of light.

'Shift now from the Shekinah, the bride of God on the tree of life, to the Kether, the crown, the Infinite Void, and dwell on the Tetragrammaton constantly.

'Shunya's work is done, from Void to Void. Blessings from Shunya in utter humility.'

Thambi said, 'Saami, all this is new to me. I don't think I can remember the...'

Shunya touched Thambi's head lightly with his right hand and said, 'Don't you worry, you'll not forget a single word that you heard just now. Like a tape recorder, you'll do the needful. Go!'

Thambi walked as fast as he could and reached the cottage of Father Joseph in twenty minutes.

Ever since he resigned from his administrative responsibilities of that of a senior bishop five years ago, Joseph Aikara lived in a single-roomed cottage in a coconut grove. Though he claimed he did not belong to the organised Church anymore, everyone still called him Father Joseph.

Living in solitude, Father Joseph continued the study of the Jewish occult text, the Kabbalah, free from organisational constraints.

That night, he had just finished his meditations and was sitting on the verandah on his old rocking chair, watching an owl getting ready to catch a mouse, when Thambi opened the gate and walked up to him.

'Namaste,' said Thambi bowing low, 'I am Thambi and I come from Tirumala where Shunya Saami lives.'

'Oh! Please come in,' said Father Joseph, 'and sit down.' He pointed to a cane armchair on the verandah.

'No, Father, I'll stand,' said Thambi but Father Joseph insisted and Thambi had to sit.

'Shunya Saami sends his greetings,' said Thambi, 'and wants me to tell you that he is going back to the Void'.

As soon as he heard this, Father Joseph's face went pale. He stood up, and uttering a shrill cry, fainted and fell backwards.

Thambi didn't know what to do. He waited patiently, sitting by his side. In a few minutes, consciousness returned and he sat up. 'I am sorry,' he said, 'and did Saami say anything else?'

Thambi told him exactly what Shunya had told him, word for word.

An ecstatic expression illumined his countenance. He bowed low and said, 'A thousand thanks for bringing this message from Saami. May the Supreme Being bless you! Tell Shunya Saami that I understand, and convey my deepest regards to him.'

'I have to go,' said Thambi and walked out of the cottage. In another twenty minutes, he was back in Shunya's cottage.

'Everything okay?' asked Shunya.

'Yes, Saami,' said Thambi and related everything that had happened.

'Good, good,' said Shunya, 'now some instructions for you. Do the breathing up and down the spine as I have shown you and fix your attention on the heart and the centre of the head. Free your mind of all thoughts and enter the Void. You have work to do.

'Now, it has been quite a taxing day for you. You need to calm your overexcited nerves. Come here and lie down on your mat.'

Thambi obeyed as always. Shunya sat beside him and softly stroked his forehead and chest. Thambi fell into deep slumber.

∾

When Sadasivan entered the house, Bhavani looked at his face and said, 'You look strange. What is it? Is Saami ill or something? Or did he scold you?'

'No, nothing,' said Sadasivan, 'I am wondering if Saami...'

'If Saami...what?'

'You know, I was thinking if Saami will always love us as he does now.'

'I have no doubt at all,' said Bhavani.

'Okay, my doubtless queen, will you get me a little gingelly oil for my head?'

'Yes, and, then?'

'Then I'll have a bath.'

'And then?'

'Then I'll eat and begin work.'

'What work?' she asked shyly.

'Up and down, in and out…'

'Chi, don't talk so loudly. Bhargavi, the maid, is in the kitchen.'

'Okay okay, hurry up.' For some strange reason he couldn't comprehend, Sadasivan couldn't bring himself to tell Bhavani what Shunya had said—that she was going to have a baby and also that he was planning to disappear forever.

After a hot water bath, Sadasivan felt a little better, but he had no appetite. He ate very little of the rice and sambar, with a small piece of dry roasted fish, and went to the bedroom.

Bhavani always ate after him. 'I'll finish my dinner, have a quick bath and come,' she said. 'You look tired but don't sleep, okay?'

Sadasivan lay on the bed thinking of Shunya and all that he had said that day. It was almost like a farewell message, parting advice. What would happen? Would he die, or just disappear?

When Bhavani came back after her bath, she found Sadasivan fast asleep.

'Must be really tired,' she said to herself, and switching off the light, slipped quietly into the bed by his side.

She didn't want to wake him up. He worked so hard,

he deserved rest. She wondered what Shunya Saami would be doing at this time in his cottage. She was on the verge of falling asleep, when she was startled by a voice whispering into her ear.

It seemed like a voice from far away. Was it Sadasivan? She wasn't sure.

Bhavani's hair stood on end but the voice was firm, so she did as she was told.

'I will give you a child. Take off your clothes.'

Bhavani closed her eyes and embraced Sadasivan. The fragrance of frankincense that she associated with her Saami wafted from her husband's body. In her mind's eye, she saw Shunya's face for a fleeting moment. Soon it was replaced by the image of her darling Krishna, the cowherd of Vrindavan, his body exuding the odour of sandalwood paste, wearing a garland of sweet-smelling flowers. He was looking lovingly at her with his lotus eyes, a beauteous smile playing on his rosy lips. A peacock feather was stuck into a jewelled headband that held his abundant, unruly black hair in place. The kaustubha jewel glistened on his chest and he was dressed in golden yellow silk garments. She surrendered.

She dared not open her eyes lest the vision vanished. She was being kissed softly and fondled, and love entered her sacred place. The orgasm was an explosion of joy that permeated every single cell of her body. A strange buzzing sound was in her ears. Suddenly, it was all over, and with her eyes still shut, she heard a voice saying, 'You will have a girl child in nine months. The child will have Shunya in her heart, the Great Nothingness. She is Shunya's gift to you. Don't look for Shunya. Shunya will go the way he came, from nowhere to nowhere.'

Bhavani opened her eyes. Sadasivan was lying beside her, naked and with his eyes closed.

Trying not to make any noise, she wrapped the saree quickly around her body, grabbed a flashlight and ran to the door. There was nobody there. The road was deserted. A lone street lamp threw its feeble light on the emptiness. But then she heard the soft and sweet music of a flute being played far away. When it stopped, she shut the door and wept uncontrollably.

37

Thambi couldn't recall when he had fallen asleep. The last thing he remembered was Shunya sitting cross-legged and stroking his forehead. When he woke up at dawn, he was gone.

Thambi went to the tap, washed his face, and waited, hoping that Shunya would walk in. When an hour passed and still Shunya was not to be seen, Thambi began to fear the worst. When Shunya had said at night that he would go out of sight soon, he hadn't thought that it would be so soon. It seemed that he was wrong. Maybe he really had gone. Maybe he was lying dead somewhere.

With mounting panic, Thambi rushed out of the cottage, and ran into the coconut grove. Shunya wasn't there. He continued walking towards the teak wood forest and beyond, over the hillock and right up to the end of the crematorium. Shunya was nowhere to be found.

Then he ran back to the pond, hoping to find Shunya emerging after his bath, but was disappointed. He asked a few people whom he met on the way. Nobody had seen Shunya. The night watchman hadn't either.

His hope that Shunya would walk in from somewhere, like magic, began to fade. Sitting inside the cottage, all alone, a strong feeling that he would never see his beloved Saami again gripped him.

Bowing down, and touching his head to the worn-out mat on which Shunya used to sit all night, Thambi began to cry loudly. Never before, not even when his dear old mother had passed away, with her head in his lap, had he cried so much. He felt orphaned.

'Thambi, where is Saami?' asked Sadasivan, standing at the open door of the cottage. His heart sank when he saw Thambi crying.

Thambi wiped his tears and stood up. He embraced Sadasivan and said, 'Sada anna, I think he is gone, sooner than we thought he would.'

Bhavani, who was standing quietly beside Sadasivan, said, 'He has gone, hasn't he? Saami is gone, I knew it. Thambi, we are orphans now,' and began to cry.

Sadasivan, always the practical man, said, 'Now we should do the needful, inform everybody and so on. Thambi, didn't Saami say he would leave something behind like Kabir, who left behind flowers?'

'Yes,' said Thambi, 'let's go and look.'

They searched the cottage and found a small cloth bundle, roughly the size of a tennis ball, in the eastern corner. It was placed on a piece of white paper with the writing, 'Here is what is left behind, nothing more there is.'

'Let's shut the door before examining it,' said Bhavani.

They shut the door, switched on the single light in the cottage, and untied the bundle. Inside was another wrapping. There were seven wrappings in all, and when the last one was untied, they saw it. A piece of dried something that looked like bull-shit.

Sadasivan and Thambi examined it closely and concluded that it was dried human excreta.

Hurriedly, they wrapped it up again.

'What do we do?' asked Sadasivan.

'I think we should preserve it,' said Thambi.

'I think we should bury it in the middle of the cottage, light a lamp over it, and build a temple,' said Bhavani. 'It is part of Saami's own body. It is holy. Let the lamp be lit perpetually.'

'But no one, except the three of us, should know what it is,' said Sadasivan. 'Thambi, before the crowds begin to gather, let's bury the holy relic. You both wait here. I'll get something to dig.'

'Thambi, do you know where Saami's flute is?' asked Bhavani.

'I couldn't find it,' said Thambi, 'maybe he took it with him.'

'Yeah, the music is also gone with him,' said Bhavani, with tears in her eyes.

In a few minutes, Sadasivan was back with a small crowbar tucked inside his shirt. He shut the door and went to work trying to make as little noise as possible. It was not difficult to dig up the red cemented floor of the cottage. In fifteen minutes, he had dug up a small pit, one foot deep and six inches in diameter.

Thambi placed the sacred object on his head first and passed it on. Bhavani and Sadasivan did the same. Then they jointly placed it with great care at the bottom of the pit, and quickly covered it with earth. Tears streaming down their faces, they pressed and levelled the earth, and plastered it with cement mixed with red oxide.

Later, Bhavani cleaned up the room and heaped golden yellow jamandhi flowers on the spot. Then placing a little oil lamp with three wicks in the centre, she lit it herself. Incense was burnt in a clay burner, and by noon the cottage was declared open to visitors.

By that time, the news had spread, and it was confirmed that Shunya had disappeared as mysteriously as he had come. Crowds of people streamed in to pay their respects. They went into the cottage and prostrated before the lamp. Thambi sat beside the lamp and meditated.

Sadasivan sat on one side with a copper pot filled with black tea, dispensing a spoonful to those visitors who asked for the sacred nectar. Bhavani sat outside the cottage, making flower garlands.

Sadasivan informed the newspapers about the dissolution of the organisation, the Saami Seva Sangam. In addition, Saami's cottage would henceforth be called the temple.

The police conducted their investigations and concluded that Shunya had wandered off to some unknown place. His name was added to the list of missing persons.

From nothingness to nothingness he had gone, but that was not the end of the saga.

38

A week after Shunya's disappearance, Diana came back to India. She married Thambi in a simple ceremony in which garlands were exchanged before Saami's lamp, as the brass lamp installed by Bhavani was called. They prostrated in front of it. Diana cried a lot thinking of Shunya Appa. 'How wonderful it would have been, Appa, if you had been here to bless us,' she said between sobs.

Being a foreign national, Diana had sent her papers to Thambi a month back and he had applied for a certificate at the local marriage registrar's office, on Shunya's orders. Now they got married officially. Then, reluctantly, she went back to England. At the airport, Bhavani applied a dot of sandalwood paste on Diana's forehead, hugged her and kissed her on the cheeks saying, 'Never forget that Saami is with you always.'

It took Thambi more than three months to get his passport. Then, in another month, he got his visa to go to England and join his spouse. Thambi and Diana settled in Sheffield and worked as teachers in a boarding school called the Pine Grove.

Sadasivan, according to the instructions of Shunya, dissolved the Saami Seva Sangam, but continued to look after the cottage which was called the temple, but only for a short time.

The land on which the cottage-temple and the toddy shop stood were not really Sadasivan's property. He had leased it out from Soman, the contractor. The politician, who had tried to get Shunya murdered, decided to exploit the situation. He paid a huge sum of money to Soman, and used his political influence to force Sadasivan to vacate the premises. Then he bought up the property.

On the pretext that he had become a devotee of Shunya, after having seen him in a dream, and that Shunya had, in the dream, asked him to build a grand temple, the old cottage was demolished. In its place, a magnificent temple of black granite was constructed. It was named the Saami Appan Vellaku Temple, which meant the Temple of the Lamp of Saami, the Father. Sadasivan gave up without protest, saying, 'If it is Saami's wish, so be it. If he wants a temple, so be it.' Bhavani cried bitterly.

Hundreds of people visited the temple. The place where the small lamp had stood was now the marble sanctum sanctorum, and there stood a five feet tall, giant brass lamp with nine wicks. No one except Thambi, Sadasivan and Bhavani knew what precious remains of Shunya lay under it.

In a niche, lit by powerful fluorescent lights, was placed a gaint blow-up of the photograph of Shunya standing under the jackfruit tree, a copy of the picture shot by Prof. Hawkins and given to Bhavani to be installed in her personal shrine. A priest was appointed to perform the service every day by ringing the bell, waving the light, lighting the incense, and distributing consecrated sweets to the devotees. Uniformed security guards controlled the crowds who came to pray and bow before the image of the great sage. The spot where the lamp stood was pointed out as the place from where the great Shunya vanished into thin air, or disappeared in a flash of light, or entered the earth which parted to receive him, and so on and so forth. Prayers of the devotees, it was claimed, were answered. The sick were healed, the poor became rich, other miracles took place, and the coffers of the temple overflowed.

The politician, who was the sole trustee of the temple, became richer than ever before. Part of his income he spent on charity with a great deal of fanfare, and was praised and admired by the general public for his goodness and philanthropic disposition. He won the elections again and remained in power.

Apart from the profit motive, he was only following the customary practice among the rich and the influential to build a temple, either as a status symbol or as a prop, to counter the negative effects of a turbulently insecure life, or to wash off their sins. It was also his way of repenting for having tried to get Shunya killed.

The monk, who had been his Guru and mentor, and one of the chief conspirators, had gone on a pilgrimage to the Himalayas soon after the unsuccessful attempt to murder Shunya. He had been crushed to death in a massive landslide. The minister was scared that some such horrible fate might befall him as well.

ॐ

Exactly ten months after Shunya's departure, a girl child was born to Bhavani. They named her Saami Nidhi, which means 'Saami's treasure'. She grew up to be a beautiful but wild girl. She refused to go to school, was blunt to the point of being abusive, and did exactly what she wanted.

She laughed often for no tangible reason, loved to climb trees and swim in the pond. Birds, squirrels, cats and dogs were her best friends.

By the time she was three years of age, the old cottage which had been converted into a little temple, had been demolished, and in its place stood the grand complex built by the politician. While Bhavani and Sadasivan visited the new temple twice a day, Nidhi refused to go there, and called it the false temple. She grew up to be tall and attractive.

One evening, at the age of fifteen, she walked out of her house, and never returned. The previous night, she had told her mother, 'Amma, I love you and Father, but Shunya, the Void-Father, is calling me. Lots of work to do.' When her mother tried to probe, she refused to say anything further on the subject. Sadasivan and Bhavani took it all calmly, and explained to others that Nidhi was Saami's child and had gone to join him. But deep inside their hearts, she had left a gaping hole, a vacuum, an emptiness, the ever-abiding state called Shunya.

They continued to stay in their old house, and visited the new temple every day. They lived quietly, readying themselves to enter the final rest. Occasionally, someone would drop in to listen to their experiences with Shunya.

Meenakshi and Salim came with their son, Deepak. The Brahmin priest's daughter, Ammini, and her husband came, bringing their daughter, Ayesha, with them.

Kunjan Namboodiri had stopped dabbling in astrology, sorcery, tantra and related practices, and dedicated his life to the study of the Hindu philosophical texts, which he claimed Shunya had commanded him to do. If anyone asked him for advice, he said, 'All is one, the great nothing is the source of all somethings. Let go and rejoice.'

One year after the disappearance of Shunya, Kunjan Namboodiri fell ill with diarrhoea and high fever. He refused to see a doctor, and on the third day, passed away with a smile on his face saying, 'Shh, don't talk. Saami is waiting to take me. Don't you hear him playing his flute? Oh! How beautiful is the music. I am coming, Shunya, here I come!' Sadasivan and Bhavani were present when he passed away. Bhavani said, 'I wish I could die like that.'

'I wish the same,' said Sadasivan.

∾

At Toddy Shop No. 423 in Jagathy, not too far from the Saami Appan temple, another matted-haired, toddy-swigging character appeared, claiming to be the new Shunya. A few months later, he was caught stealing money from the cash box of the toddy shop but was let off with a minor warning. But when it was discovered that he was a confirmed paedophile, and had molested half-a-dozen children of the local school by enticing them with chocolates, he was severely thrashed by the public.

He ran away, and was never heard of again.

Meanwhile, far away, on a quiet beach near Kanjankaad, a fishing village close to the border of coastal Karnataka, a naked teenaged girl, tall and attractive, with dark complexion and long black tresses, appeared one golden morning. A pack of ten mongrels of all colours, shapes and sizes followed her wherever she went, and formed a gnarling security cordon around her the moment anyone tried to approach her. An old fisherwoman, who took the risk of trying again and again, was rewarded by being invited by the strange girl to come close. Ordered by her, the dogs quietened down, and let her pass.

'Who are you?' was the first question the old woman asked. 'Shunya,' was the reply.

She refused to answer any more questions. After a few minutes of silence, she smiled and unexpectedly hugged the fisherwoman warmly, muttering, 'Poor thing. Enter the Void and enjoy the bliss of the great Vagina. You are free, enjoy, enjoy.'

Something akin to an electric current entered the old lady's heart. Drunk with ecstasy, she ran back to her home in the fishing village, shouting at the top of her voice, 'Come and enjoy, all of you! Shunyamma, the great Godess, has come to bless us.' That was when she realised that she had done the impossible: run a whole mile, when just an hour ago, crippled by arthritis, she could hardly walk. She had been cured by the hug.

That evening, Shunyamma received her first meal from the village. It was a simple meal of fish curry and tapioca brought by the old woman, Ponnamma, and her daughter and son-in-law. From that day on, the feeding became a daily ritual. Shunyamma ate with relish, and shared the food with her canine companions.

As days went by, others began to come to get a glimpse of the naked saint, first in a trickle, and as the fantastic stories of their experiences spread, the trickle swelled to a wave. In a year's time, Shunyamma, as she was now known, was visited by hundreds of people, rich and poor. Still, no one knew who she was and where she had come from.

A house was being built by those who called themselves her devotees. She took one look at it and said, 'Shit, this is a shit place. Shunya will not stay here.' She continued to sleep in an old, abandoned, thatched shack, with her dogs beside her. When the rains came it leaked badly, but neither she nor her dogs seemed to care. The foul language she used, the carefree life she led, and her habitual nudity made her a darling of the media.

And so her fame grew day by day, with people swarming to catch a glimpse of this new goddess, who revealed all without reservation. Some came to have her darshan, some expecting a cure, some hoping for genuine spiritual upliftment, and some out of mere curiosity.

One night it rained heavily with deafening thunder and lightning. That night, she disappeared and was never seen again.

The next morning, Sadasivan and Bhavani, having seen the media reports and sure that Shunyamma was certainly their daughter gifted by Saami, came looking for her. But it was too late. They returned home empty-handed. The void remained in their hearts and eventually expanded to become the blissful, all-pervading Void.

39

A remarkable change had come over M.K. when Shunya, after rising from his death-like trance, had touched him on his head. M.K never went back home. Instead, he got onto a bus and travelled twenty miles to reach an isolated beach called Vizhinjam, where an old lighthouse stood, which had for many years guided boats and ships from the turbulent sea to the shore.

There, he walked on the sands until he came close to the water. The full moon shed its cool, silvery light, and the powerful beam of the lighthouse's rotating beacon flashed at regular intervals. Sitting down, he stretched his legs and let the cold water of the breaking waves wash his feet. That was when he heard the soft, soothing strains of a flute being played somewhere close by.

Drawn irresistibly to the music, he got up and ran here and there like a madman, trying to find the source. It seemed to come from a small rockery. M.K. climbed up the rocks, and there he found to his great astonishment, Shunya, leaning against the gnarled stump of an old tree, playing his flute. Shunya's eyes were closed.

M.K. squatted on the sand in front of Shunya, closed his eyes, and forgot the world. On the wings of the rainbow-hued symphony, he flew softly across the chasm of dualistic thought, and merged with the supramental Void, the darkness which is the mother of light.

He came back to earth when he heard his name being called, as if from far away. Opening his eyes, he saw Shunya sitting in the Buddha posture. Waves of bliss, Shunya, the Great Void, washed over him.

'You are ripe now,' said Shunya, and walked away.

From that day M.K. lived on the beach, retiring at night to the rockery, wandering on the sands at daytime, come rain or scorching sunshine. He had stopped talking, and wore a dirty loincloth which often slipped down his waist.

The fishermen, who lived nearby, fed him whenever they felt sorry for him, but they had to sometimes brave the volley of sand and stones which he aimed at those who dared to go near him too often. His face was always ecstatic as if he was enjoying something unknown to the others. His hair and beard became long and matted, and he looked and acted like a madman.

But there was someone who dared to go and sit near him, a six-year-old fisher-boy, an orphan called Mathias. Soon, he became a kind of constant companion to M.K. He brought M.K. food and water, massaged his feet, played with him, building sand castles, and as he grew older, began to spend whole days and nights with him every now and then.

No one had heard them talk to each other, and no one knew what passed between them. The relationship continued even after Mathias grew up to become a young man. He borrowed money from the local money-lender, bought himself a fishing boat, then a trawler. Quickly climbing the ladder of success, Mathias became a wealthy fisherman.

M.K. died quietly one night, lying on the sands of Vizhinjam beach, his feet touching the water. Mathias was then twenty-five years old. He buried M.K near the rockery which had been his abode, and built a simple tomb. On it was installed a wooden cross with the epitaph: Here lies my father, mother and God. Praise be to Jesus.

From that time till the ripe old age of eighty-nine when he passed away peacefully, Mathias used his wealth to support a number of orphanages and schools for the poor, and was known as the man who never hurt anyone. He never got married.

Some said that he was a disciple of M.K., but when asked, he merely smiled and said, 'I don't know, but M.K. was my father, mother and friend.'

40

In Sheffield, England, Thambi and Diana continued teaching at the Pine Grove School. With Prof. Hawkin's help, Thambi's notebook was printed for private circulation with the title, *Living with Shunya: Sage of the Tavern*. Copies of the book were distributed free to those who were interested. Eventually, a small group was formed, which met on the last Sunday of every month to discuss the book. The group remained small for a long time.

Prof. Hawkins kept in touch. He travelled to England twice every year to stay with them. Whenever he came, a gathering was organised, where he would talk about his association with 'Zero Dad', as the group loved to call Shunya. One of his favourite stories was about his friend Timothy Davies, the librarian who had introduced him to Shunya in the first place.

After Bob had returned to the US, he had tried to get in touch with Timmy to thank him. He was told over the telephone by Timmy's sister that one evening, a week back, a stranger who Timmy seemed to be on friendly terms with, and who looked like an Indian yogi, had walked into their study, and had gone for a walk with her brother after a cup of tea. He had spoken to her in English and had said that they were going for a long stroll.

They never came back. She had informed the police after waiting for a day. That was the last anyone heard of Timothy Davies. He had merged with the Void.

41

Prof. Hawkins distributed Thambi's book to a select group of his associates and friends, and talked about his own experiences with Shunya to those who were inclined to listen. One of his friends who received the book was Dr Jacob Mathews.

Dr Jacob was a professor of neurology, and the one of the few men of science who evinced interest in what is called neurotheology, a subject frowned upon by the scientific establishment in general. Neurotheologians hypothesised that the brain was possibly wired for experiencing altered states of consciousness, and employed various techniques, including brain-scanning, to investigate the brains of meditators, epileptics and others who claimed to have paranormal experiences.

Of Indian origin, Dr Jacob, though born of orthodox Christian parents, was deeply interested in yoga and Hindu philosophy since childhood. Prof. Hawkins had known him for several years, ever since he had come to the US. Dr Jacob had immigrated to New York after a five-year stint as the head of an institute on neurological sciences at Ranchi, in India. Prof. Hawkins and Dr Jacob stayed in touch and exchanged notes frequently.

One evening, as Dr Jacob flipped through the pages of *Living with Shunya*, Shunya's photograph caught his eye. Faint memories were stirred within him. There seemed to be some connection between the man in the photograph and his days in Ranchi. When and where had he seen him? It could be my imagination, he said to himself, as he read the book. It was fascinating. He couldn't put it down. He read the whole night and finished it by four in the morning. Then he switched off the reading light and lay in bed, thinking deeply.

Most neurologists and psychiatrists would have branded Shunya a typical schizophrenic, but Dr Jacob thought differently. So much wisdom and so strange a life, he said to himself. Wasn't Shunya's behaviour considered abnormal because it differed from the so-called standardised behaviour patterns of the majority? Maybe for Shunya the normal was abnormal. Schizophrenics were split personalities, but were there any unsplit personalities? Everybody was a split personality to a certain extent—only in some, the dichotomy between the parts was pronounced.

Dr Jacob had a theory. Perhaps brain centres which were dormant in most humans functioned actively in certain people, providing insights into dimensions that are ordinarily unknown. But theories needed proof, and...just a minute, that typical Ho Chi Minh beard, the penetrating eyes—now he remembered.

One morning, many years ago, while he was working in Ranchi, a middle-aged patient was brought to him, clad in a white loincloth, clutching a flute in his hand, looking fully drunk and behaving strangely. He had impressive degrees in science from Indian and foreign universities, and was amazingly learned in matters pertaining to religion and philosophy. He claimed to be nothing, Shunya, the Void. It was so long ago, and some other doctor had taken over the case...

Into the nameless zone, Jacob drifted. No doctor, no patient, no, he wasn't falling asleep, it was something else. The incessant chatter of the mind ceased spontaneously, and an all-embracing, multi-dimensional rainbow lit the inner chamber of his heart. A flute played far away, sweet music, a lover's call, a soft whisper, the beloved's response, gentle jasmine-scented breeze, sssh! Don't use words… silence. He entered the Void, the Shunya.

Acknowledgements

First and foremost, I acknowledge the unseen hand of my mentor, Babaji, in guiding me to do all that I do.

Next, I acknowledge the contribution of my dear friends and associates who in ways, seen and unseen, helped me create something out of nothing—Shunya—and see beauty in what sometimes appears empty and insignificant.

Last but not the least, those friends of mine who were convinced that Shunya is worth writing a novel about.